"This isn't a wedding, it's a publicity stunt!"

Holly winced as she saw the photographers gathered outside the church.

Laurel turned to her sister. "Jack and I are beginning our new life together. We want the world to know."

The driver opened her door and Laurel climbed out of the limousine. "Come on. I don't want to keep Jack waiting!"

Laurel smiled into a blizzard of flashes and started up the steps, her veil billowing behind her.

Jack moved toward her. One look at him and Laurel forgot all about the photographers and her sisters. There was only her handsome soon-to-be husband holding out his hand to her.

"I love that dress," he whispered. "But not nearly as much as I love the woman who's wearing it."

Dear Reader,

My own wedding was extremely different from Laurel's. I'm very traditional. And red clashes with my hair.

There were fireworks, literally, when I married my high school sweetheart at 8:00 p.m. on the Fourth of July, with my ten-year-old sister as maid of honor. My mother had designed and sewn my wedding dress, I carried a blue-beaded rose from my grandmother's wedding suit and had the same sixpence rattling in my shoe that rattled in my mother's on her wedding day. The family dachshund wore the bridal garter.

I wanted (why didn't someone talk me out of it?) an outdoor reception. In Houston. In July. The heat, humidity and mosquitoes might be a problem, but at least we wouldn't have to worry about rain. It never rains on the Fourth of July.

And it hasn't since my wedding day. But if it hadn't rained, I would have missed the rainbow. My bridesmaids and I, electric curlers in our hair, had piled into the family car and were on our way to the church. In one of those glorious moments straight out of a movie script, the setting sun broke through the clouds and a full double rainbow appeared over the freeway, just about where the church was.

We weren't the only ones to see the rainbow, and during the soggy reception, people told us it was a sign. A sign of what, they didn't say. Personally, I think it was a warning never to plan outdoor parties during Houston summers. The heavens had relented once—but we shouldn't press our luck. And we haven't.

I hope you enjoy reading Laurel's story. She and her sisters first appeared in *Deck the Halls* and have been reunited in *Jack of Hearts*. You'll meet the Hall family again in my next book, *Ivy's League*.

Sincerely,

Heather Allison

JACK OF HEARTS
Heather Allison

Harlequin Books

TORONTO • NEW YORK • LONDON
AMSTERDAM • PARIS • SYDNEY • HAMBURG
STOCKHOLM • ATHENS • TOKYO • MILAN
MADRID • WARSAW • BUDAPEST • AUCKLAND

To my little sister, Allison Wilkes,
whose name appears on the spine of this book.
Remember, you've got to kiss a lot of frogs
before you find a prince.

I'm indebted to Dale Friend for his help in
making the poker scenes as authentic as possible.
Thanks, and may you draw a royal flush
in a high-stakes game.

ISBN 0-373-03218-8

Harlequin Romance first edition September 1992

JACK OF HEARTS

CHAPTER ONE

LAUREL HALL'S TAXI sped down the large circular drive-way in the exclusive Highland Park area of Dallas and squeaked to a stop in front of a palatial, white-columned house.

"That'll be twenty-three eighty," announced the driver.

Laurel went through the motions of digging in her purse, gradually increasing the tempo of her movements. "My billfold!" Just the right touch of disbelief and despera-tion, she thought.

The cabbie obviously wasn't impressed, but Laurel couldn't waste her best performance on him. *That* she'd save for her family. "Wait here."

He shrugged and flipped on the radio. "'Deck the halls with boughs of holly...'"

Laurel sighed heavily. Of all the Christmas carols to hear on her ignominious return home... She ran up the three steps and stopped in front of the door. Should she ring the doorbell? She assumed it had been fixed sometime in the nearly three years since she'd lived here.

Laurel punched the bell. Almost immediately, the door opened, and she faced her brother-in-law's searing blue eyes.

Drat. Holly and Ivy, her sisters, would have made soothing noises as they paid the cabbie while Laurel sobbed out a stolen-wallet story.

But Adam...Adam would immediately suspect that she hadn't had anything to steal in the first place. Well, shouldn't two years of acting lessons be good for something?

"Hi, Adam! Uh..." What she needed now was a good script.

"Laurel! Thanks for coming. I—"

The cabbie beeped his horn.

Adam's glance flicked over Laurel in quick appraisal, shifted to the cab, then returned to her for a much slower study.

Laurel knew he saw a thinner, darker-haired version of the Laurel who had left Dallas for Hollywood.

Double drat. Adam would figure out in moments what she had spent two years denying even to herself.

Laurel Hall was a failure. "Adam, I—"

"It's okay." Adam touched her briefly on the shoulder, then ran lightly down the steps and paid the cabbie. "Luggage?" he called.

Laurel barely moved her head in a quick shake of denial. Everything she'd brought from California—an extra T-shirt, underwear and a little black dress—was in the denim hobo bag slung over her shoulder.

She managed to meet Adam's eyes as he climbed the steps. When he reached the porch, he stopped and stared at her.

Laurel braced herself for one of Adam's hard, assessing gazes. He always saw more than she would have liked, but was scrupulously fair, too. He'd even taken her side when she decided to quit her sisters' Christmas decorating service, Deck the Halls, and try her luck at becoming an actress.

"My luggage has been lost." Laurel hoped Adam would assume that the airline had lost it. Actually, she'd sold her bags months ago; sooner or later, she'd traded or sold everything of value.

Adam didn't ask her which airline as she had thought he would. And that was fine, since she'd taken the bus. Hard to lose luggage on a bus. "Any chance of finding it?"

"No."

He knew; she could tell. Without another word, Adam reached an arm around her shoulders and pulled her close as they walked into the house.

Did Holly realize how lucky she was to have someone like Adam? Someone to lean on?

"Holly's in the kitchen."

Laurel nodded and sniffed as she straightened.

"We redecorated." Adam gestured to the front room, giving Laurel a chance to collect herself. She knew there would be no prying questions or I-told-you-so's from him.

"This looks more like a reception area," she commented, taking in the phone, desk, filing cabinets and waiting-room atmosphere.

"That's the idea. Holly sees Deck the Halls clients here. We converted several of the bedrooms—I use those for my legal clients. I act as a mediator exclusively now, and meeting in a home setting tends to calm people." He smiled gently.

Laurel tilted up her chin, warning him with a look that she could stand gentleness, but not pity.

The quiet in the foyer—in the whole house—amazed her. This close to Christmas, she remembered, the mansion was usually the site of frantic activity as she and her sisters scrambled to pack ornaments for various tree-decorating jobs they'd landed. Their whole standard of living depended on the Christmas season. Laurel knew Holly had continued Deck the Halls after she and Ivy had left home, but where were the boxes? The carts? The inventory sheets? The shouting and screaming?

As she and Adam walked to the kitchen, Laurel felt surprisingly nervous. What could she, who had nothing, say to Holly, who now had everything?

"Laurel!" Ivy, her younger sister, raced down the front staircase and waylaid her. Adam grinned and walked into the other room as Laurel hugged her.

"Look at you!" Ivy gave her a once-over, too, but apparently didn't see what Adam had seen. "Wow! You're so thin! And what did you do to your hair?"

Outwardly, Laurel smiled. "I dyed it black to audition for the role of a Gypsy."

"Did you get the part?" Ivy asked eagerly.

"No."

"Well, I'm glad. Otherwise, you couldn't have come home, right?"

"Yeah," Laurel echoed. "Otherwise I wouldn't have come home."

"Look." Ivy dragged her over to the hall mirror. The black dye had faded, making Laurel's hair a close match to Ivy's dark brown. Ivy, still a college journalism student, wore her hair long and straight. Laurel's hair was long now, too. Cheaper to maintain.

Ivy pointed. "We actually look like sisters for once."

They did, except Ivy didn't have rings under her brown eyes or minute wrinkles at the outer corners. She looked fresh. Laurel looked shopworn.

"I expected boxes of tree decorations everywhere. Isn't business any good this year?" Laurel asked, turning away from the painful reflection in the mirror.

"Deck the Halls is bigger than ever, but Holly hires lots of part-timers," Ivy explained as they walked toward the kitchen. "They work upstairs."

"And just how many people does it take to replace us?"

"Twelve," Ivy said with a grin. "That gives her four teams of three each."

"Maybe I should have stuck around."

"Are you kidding?" Ivy looked at her with an admiring expression. "Acting in movies is better than selling Christmas-tree designs."

"Acting isn't as glamorous as you think." Laurel had been in precisely one movie, a low-budget horror flick, which had gone directly to the video-rental stores. She'd played the part of a sorority-girl corpse dressed in lingerie she never would have considered wearing when she'd been a *live* sorority girl.

Although she'd given the director the benefit of her experience, he had not appreciated her input.

Laurel's total screen time was less than three seconds.

At first, she'd thought the two events were related. Now she knew she had been such an insignificant nobody that the director, rather insignificant himself, wouldn't have made the effort to sabotage her nonexistent career.

She squared her shoulders and stepped into the kitchen.

"Laurel! I'm so glad you're..."

Laurel braced for a hug that didn't happen. "Holly?"

A curly-headed woman with a stunned expression sat at the kitchen table, spoon poised above a container of Blue Bell Caramel Turtle Fudge ice cream.

Laurel's stomach rumbled. Breakfast had been two foil packages of ketchup dissolved in hot water; Laurel had heard that tomatoes were a good source of vitamin C.

"You're...you're so thin!" Holly's face crumpled. "And I'm so faaat!" The word ended on a wail as Holly began sobbing into her ice cream.

"Not again," Ivy moaned beside Laurel.

Laurel blinked in disbelief. *This* was her determinedly competent, relentlessly driven older sister? The same sister who'd fought legions of lawyers when their father's death had left his business in a shambles? The same woman who had supported them all?

"What have you done to her?" She directed her question toward her brother-in-law. Adam wore a pained expression and moved tortilla chips and hot sauce out of Holly's reach.

Holly emotional? Holly snacking? Holly—well, it had to be said—*pudgy?* Suddenly understanding, Laurel smiled. "Congratulations, Adam," she said above Holly's sobs. "When are you gonna be a daddy?"

"Not soon enough," he muttered.

"I heard that!"

"Holly..." Adam looked helpless.

Laurel enjoyed the sight. Her brother-in-law had never been helpless in his life.

"You don't love me anymore!"

"Yes, I do!"

But he spoke just a shade too forcefully, and Holly began to wail again. "How could you? I'm blimp-woman."

"I may not last until Christmas," Ivy said in an undertone.

"Their *marriage* may not last until Christmas."

"She missed her nap 'cause she wanted to be awake when you got here," Ivy whispered.

Laurel widened her eyes. "She takes a nap?"

Ivy held up two fingers.

Laurel raised an eyebrow. "Things *have* changed."

"Holly, listen." Ivy read from a book that had been sitting on the counter. "'The healthy pregnant woman should gain between three and five pounds during the first trimester...'" Ivy trailed off at Adam's frantic signaling.

Too late.

"I've gained nine!" Holly pushed away the soggy Blue Bell carton.

"Doesn't that book also mention getting plenty of rest?" Laurel prompted.

"Oh, yes." Ivy nodded. "*Lots* of rest, Holly."

"I *am* tired," Holly admitted as Adam helped her out of the chair and toward the door.

"How far along is she?" Laurel asked, eyeing Holly's baggy sweater as she shuffled past.

"A couple of months."

"That's *all?*" The sisters looked at each other and began to laugh. "Poor Holly," Ivy said.

"Poor Adam," Laurel replied, casually wandering over to the counter where Adam had placed the tortilla chips.

Her hands shook and the plastic bag crackled. She forced herself to keep her movements slow and controlled as she grabbed a handful of chips.

"Something to drink?" Ivy offered, opening the door to the refrigerator.

"Sure." Laurel began to munch the chips, savoring the salt, careful not to swallow too fast.

Adam wandered back into the kitchen and stood beside the door, silently observing.

Laurel carried the bag of chips to the kitchen table and sat down. Moments later, Adam put a thick sandwich in front of her.

"Thanks," she said, making sure he knew it was for more than just preparing the sandwich. Whatever he suspected, he was keeping it to himself.

"Boy, I'm glad you're here," Ivy sighed, stealing some of Laurel's chips. "Holly's been impossible ever since she found out about Conner Mathison."

"That's a name out of the past." He had been one of her father's associates and poker-playing buddies. Maybe not a buddy. "Buddy" didn't fit the urbane, silver-haired Conner.

"He was a partner in several of your father's ventures," Adam supplied, sitting at the table with them. "One of which was the well in west Texas."

"The . . . the one that caught fire?" The one her parents had been flying to when their plane crashed, causing the world Laurel had known to crash with it.

Both Ivy and Adam nodded.

"I thought everything had finally been settled." Laurel didn't like this. She was sick of legal battles, even though Holly had dealt with most of them. "What have you found out?"

Ivy leaned forward, wearing a hard expression that didn't belong on her young face. "Holly's been decorating a lot of society parties and heard some very interesting stories about Conner."

Laurel looked to Adam for confirmation. "Such as?"

"We did some checking and—"

Ivy interrupted her brother-in-law. "We think he set the well on fire so he could collect the insurance money to pay off gambling debts."

A roaring filled Laurel's eyes. "But...everyone said Dad set the fire! They said his business was failing." She'd never believed her father was capable of being so dishonorable.

"Conner—"

"Or someone," Adam interjected.

"Conner," repeated Ivy more forcefully, "embezzled money. Dad never knew."

Food, usually uppermost in Laurel's mind, was forgotten. "But Dad must have known the business was in trouble—"

"And it was. But we're sure Conner cooked the books, too. He's the only person who could have. Don't you remember how there wasn't any money at all? Don't you think Dad would have held *something* back for us?"

It was as if the curtain of time had been drawn aside, and Laurel could see the events of eight years ago, through the eyes of an adult.

She glanced at Adam, who spoke. "Conner did have the opportunity. As a partner, he had access to your father's office. And you know your father was struggling. During all the confusion after the crash..." Adam shrugged.

"And remember—" Ivy raised a finger "—Conner bought an insurance policy on that well, Dad didn't."

A blinding, white-hot anger ripped through Laurel. They'd endured humiliation after humiliation. The contents of their home had been auctioned, laid out for everyone to paw over. She and her sisters had worked long hours to survive. They'd been abandoned by friends, betrayed by businesspeople and hounded by lawyers. And now it seemed all their suffering had been caused by one man—Conner Mathison.

"Why didn't anyone figure this out before now?" Laurel demanded accusingly of Adam. "Why didn't anyone suspect him?"

"Because Conner Mathison is a very, very good liar. But by all accounts—and there are a lot of them—he's a serious gambler."

Ivy jumped up and plucked a book from a tall stack on the phone table. "*Psychology of the Compulsive Gambler* says, 'Lying is more natural than telling the truth.

They lie even when they don't have to.' That's one of the phases of being a compulsive gambler."

"I'll admit the rest fits, too." Adam leaned forward. "When a gambler loses, he begins acquiring money any way he can."

"So who do we tell about Conner?" Laurel looked from Adam to Ivy. They'd been right to ask her to come home. Holly couldn't handle more legal battles, her pregnancy and the Christmas season all at once. Ivy, home for the holidays, would have to return to school in a month. Adam had a thriving legal-mediation firm. They *needed* Laurel.

This time she wouldn't let them down.

Adam took a deep breath, the kind people take when they're about to tell you something you don't want to hear. "I approached the attorney general. He declined to prosecute."

Laurel pushed the sandwich away. She should eat, but she couldn't. She thought of her parents, of her big jovial father, always ready to help a friend. And of her mother, who had her own reserves of quiet strength. Who'd sold the diamonds from her spectacular necklace rather than see her family sink too deeply into debt.

A warm, masculine hand covered hers. "I told Holly, and I'm telling you, to let go of your anger. Anger and bitterness will eat away at you, and there's nothing we can do now."

"Oh, yes, there is," said a voice from the doorway. Holly stood there, riffling a pack of cards.

"I thought you were going to take a nap." Adam leveled an accusing look at her.

"How can I sleep when my sister just came home? Besides, I don't trust you and Ivy to explain the plan properly."

"Plan?" Laurel asked.

Holly tossed the cards onto the middle of the kitchen table. "We, or rather you, Laurel, are going to beat Conner Mathison at his own game." She took a seat. "Which we've heard," she said, shuffling the cards, "is poker."

"Wait a minute, wait . . . a . . . minute." Laurel stared at her sisters. "Are you telling me you called me home to play poker against Conner Mathison? *That's* your plan?"

"At least we waited until we *had* a plan," Ivy said.

"And it *is* Christmas." Holly began to deal. "You haven't been home for the last two." Her innocent expression belied the hint of accusation in her voice.

Laurel remembered Adam's voice on the phone. He'd sounded worried, though he'd tried to hide it. She glanced at him now and found him watching Holly closely.

Her sister must be burning with frustration. Laurel was, and she'd never been as closely involved with the legal mess her father had left as Holly had been.

Laurel sighed. "I've played very little poker since Dad let me sit in on his Wednesday-night games," she warned.

"So you're a teensy bit rusty. Let's play a hand of two." Holly pointed to the pile of cards in front of Laurel.

"Daddy said you were good," Ivy assured her.

"I was never good enough to beat Conner."

"That's why we got all these books for you." Ivy began reading titles of the books stacked by the telephone. "I've got *How to Play Winning Poker, Win at Poker, Winner Poker, The Poker Winner, Poker Strategy* and *America's Favorite Game.*"

"I thought that last was something else," drawled Laurel. It felt good to revert to her Texas drawl after trying to remember to sound all the consonants and speed up the vowels.

"You mean football?" Ivy asked.

"No, honey." Laurel arranged her cards, deciding that it would be easier to demonstrate her inability rather than argue with her sisters.

She won the hand.

"You see!" Holly was triumphant. "Conner is doomed. Here, Ivy, your deal."

No wonder Adam had called Laurel. Holly had finally flipped. "Pregnancy has affected more than just your waistline." Laurel stared at the cards Ivy dealt. "Holly, honey, as frustrated as I am, I'm not about to devote my life to chasing Conner in poker games."

"Only one game." Holly clenched her jaw and darted a resentful look at Adam. "Adam made me promise. But it'll be a humdinger of a game. We're going to win all his money. Without cheating. I won't fight on his level." She studied her hand.

Laurel glanced at Adam. "Hormones," he mouthed.

"I saw that." Holly slammed her cards on the table. "I can't say anything without you accusing me of being the victim of rampaging hormones!" Her voice rose. "I want to beat Conner—just once—so he'll know what it feels like to lose to us."

"How will that change anything?" Laurel asked. She was intrigued by this new emotional Holly. Her admiration for her brother-in-law's patience increased.

"I don't want Dad's first grandchild to grow up thinking that we didn't try to get even—"

"Holly," warned Adam.

"I didn't say revenge," Holly pointed out.

"That's what you say to me," Ivy murmured.

"It's just . . . Oh, I don't know." Holly slumped in the chair.

"I do," Ivy inserted quietly. "When you tell your child this story, you want an ending. 'The statute of limitations ran out' is not an ending. 'Auntie Laurel challenged the villain to a poker game and won' is."

Laurel smiled. It made sense in a Holly-kind of way. Besides, Auntie Laurel as heroine appealed to her. It would probably be the only time she'd ever play the lead. "Okay," she said, deciding that striking back at Conner might ease this helpless frustration they all felt. "Hand me one of your books, Ivy. Pick up your cards, Holly. Let's see how much practice I need."

However, after two hours of playing, she discovered that she needed a lot more than practice. "This isn't going to work."

"Maybe, if we played for M&M's instead of pinto beans..." Holly suggested longingly.

"No." Laurel shook her head. "I need real help."

"I'm looking into it." Adam sighed. "And I'm sorry I am."

Laurel chuckled at his exasperated look. "Now why is that, Adam, honey?"

"Because—"

"Because you don't want me *upsetting* myself, right?" Holly asked, a dangerous tone in her voice.

Ivy winced and scrunched down in her chair. Adam visibly braced himself.

Laurel stepped into the breach. "Which should show you how much he loves you, in spite of the fact that you've been acting completely unlovable."

"But I'm serious about this!" Holly's lip quivered.

"You're allowed a certain amount of leeway because of your condition," Laurel went on.

"I'm not sick, I'm pregnant!"

"If you continue to work yourself into a hissy fit every time you think of that skunk Conner Mathison, you *will* make yourself sick."

Holly's eyes widened, but her lip stopped quivering.

Ivy and Adam were listening attentively to Laurel. She felt some of the old self-confidence, beaten out of her in Hollywood, return. "You don't need to worry about Conner. Worry about my niece or nephew. *I'll* worry about Conner." She turned to her brother-in-law. "Now, what's this help you're working on?"

Adam's resigned expression drew a smile from her. "One of my fraternity brothers, Jack Hartman, was quite a card player when we were in school. He regularly played in high-stakes games. He was a freshman the year I was a senior."

"Did I meet him at your wedding?" Laurel asked.

"No. Jack is, or was, a stockbroker and couldn't get away." Adam's brow wrinkled. "I'm having a little trouble tracking him down. He's no longer with the same brokerage firm, and his mother tells me he's holed up in their fishing cabin."

"A hermit card shark?" Holly looked doubtful.

"Not the Jack I remember," Adam said in a concerned tone. "I left a message with the owner of a bait shop near the cabin. His mother says he checks in there every so often and gives her a call."

"He certainly ought to call his own mother at Christmas," Ivy said.

"He might have trouble getting a plane ticket until after New Year's. Were the flights crowded, Laurel?" Holly asked.

Laurel stared at her older sister. *Admit everything now,* urged a voice inside her. *Tell them you spent your last dollar on a bus ticket to Dallas and haven't eaten in two days. Tell them you've quit. Tell them and get it over with.*

She hesitated, remembering how they'd listened to her earlier. Especially Holly. Something inside Laurel warmed when she thought of gaining her sisters' respect and admiration. They loved her, of course, but they'd never really looked up to her—except insofar as she was the tallest of the three.

Before she could admit that she had no idea how difficult it would be to get an airplane ticket, Adam spoke. "Jack'll get here as soon as he can. He owes me a favor."

Meeting her brother-in-law's steady gaze, Laurel telegraphed a silent thanks. Now *she* owed him a favor, too.

CHAPTER TWO

FAVOR OR NOT, Laurel thought early the next morning, she didn't expect to see this Jack person for days. And until he arrived, she had other worries, such as how she was going to buy presents for everyone when she didn't have a single cent. She had concentrated so much on getting home that she hadn't even considered Christmas shopping.

The laundry-room tile felt cold to her bare feet. Shivering, Laurel stuffed her jeans, T-shirt and underwear into the washing machine. She wore her only other change of clothing—her audition dress, a black, sleeveless, scooped-neck mini. It hadn't always been a mini, but the dress was made of rayon, and Laurel had thought she could save on dry-cleaning expenses by carefully hand washing it. The dress had shrunk, but so had she, and it fit better now, after all.

The doorbell rang just as she started the washing machine. She ran to answer it before the ringing awakened anyone.

"Jack Hartman, here as requested." A man with the familiar Northeastern accent of her brother-in-law lifted his hand in a lazy salute. Looking over his shoulder, Laurel saw a custom-painted blue Jaguar sitting in the circular drive.

"Where's the panic?" He tossed a soft carry-on bag through the doorway without waiting for an invitation.

"Panic?" Laurel immediately categorized Adam's friend as a cocky Young Turk. He looked like he'd stepped out of an L.L. Bean catalog. Photogenic good looks were deliberately roughened by several days' growth of beard. Square-cut jaw, gleaming white teeth. She knew the type— Model Mike goes on location.

"Yeah. Adam called in an old debt." Jack didn't look at her as he spoke. Laurel watched him scan the spacious interior of her home before he lifted two pieces of designer luggage and used his Top-Sider-clad foot to nudge a third over the threshold. "Feel free to lend a hand."

"Do come in," Laurel said with exaggeration.

"*There's* that Southern hospitality I've heard so much about."

"Inspired by a glorious example of Yankee charm," Laurel replied.

Jack dropped his suitcases and sighed. "I told Adam last night I wasn't fit to be around humans."

"You were right."

He turned then, a corner of his mouth tilting as he slumped onto one of the suitcases. "You're not Holly, are you?"

Laurel shook her head and decided to yank Jack's bag the rest of the way inside so she could shut the door.

"Can't see Adam married to you." Laurel noticed he spoke to her legs and immediately straightened. "You're not his type."

Privately, Laurel agreed with Jack, but she was the one who decided whether a man was her type or not. "Neither are you."

Jack absorbed her barb without so much as the flicker of an eyelid. "You another stray who's here for the holidays?"

"No," Laurel said evenly. Pretty boys couldn't get to her. "I'm Laurel, Holly's sister."

"You're the one I'm supposed to teach to play poker." Jack blinked, as if he were adjusting a mental picture. "Jack Hartman," he said again and held out his hand.

Laurel took it automatically, finding that Jack didn't have a pretty boy's grip.

She felt energy as real as the static radiating from a television picture tube—right before she got shocked. Energy hummed through him, surrounded him, and when she gazed into his pale green eyes—money-colored eyes—she saw it burning in them.

Uneasy, Laurel tried to tug her hand away, but to her surprise, Jack held it and reached for her other one.

He turned the palms up, and for a brief instant, Laurel thought he was going to kiss them.

Rubbing his thumbs over her calluses, he asked, "What kind of work do you do, Laurel?"

"I'm an actress," she answered, then remembered that she'd decided to quit.

Jack flipped her palms down and studied the backs of her hands. Laurel curled her fingers, but Jack spread them out and looked up at her.

"Waitressing?" He tapped the minute burns hot grease had left on her skin.

"Yeah." Laurel snatched her hands away. "So?"

"Honest work. Why are you ashamed?"

And she'd thought Adam was uncanny at reading people.

How she felt was none of Jack's business, and she had no intention of discussing her feelings with him. She opened her mouth to deny that she was ashamed of working as a waitress while she attended acting classes and auditioned for parts.

Jack had laced his fingers together and was dangling them between his knees. She had his complete attention; in fact, he seemed truly interested in her answer.

It was intoxicating, being the object of someone's complete attention. It occurred to Laurel that most people were thinking of other things or doing other things or were preparing to do other things while they carried on conversations.

"Here." Jack patted the other suitcase. "Your feet probably hurt. Mine always did when I waited tables."

Her feet *did* hurt. In two years, they'd grown a size wider and a half-size longer. Her ostrich-skin boots, her pride and joy, no longer fit. Though that hadn't stopped her from wearing them on the long trip home.

Laurel sat on the suitcase, noting the rich leather and designer initials. She gestured to the luggage. "It's been a long time since you waited tables."

"Yeah, but I've never been ashamed ... of waiting tables. Would have preferred to be doing something else at the time, but I wasn't ashamed."

"Well, I was!" The outburst caught Laurel by surprise. She hadn't intended to tell this man anything.

"Why?"

"Because I was supposed to be acting!"

"You're a has-been, huh?"

Laurel swallowed. Hard. Hard enough to squeeze down a lump full of quivers. "Nope. I'm a never-was."

She saw Jack's eyes skim the contours of her face. "Did you give it everything you had?"

Laurel blinked and stared at her blistered feet. She'd earned every one of those blisters. "Yes." She lifted her head and looked Jack right in his cool green eyes. "Yes, I did."

The green eyes held approval. "There isn't one person in ten who would admit to trying flat out to do something and coming up short. They'd have all sorts of excuses."

Laurel sniffed derisively and looked away again. "I made excuses, all right. I made them to myself."

Jack slipped off the suitcase and maneuvered himself into her line of sight. "Doing your best is all anyone can ask of you, and it's all you can ask of yourself."

Laurel shook her head. "My best wasn't good enough."

His face held the same concern she'd seen on Adam's face when he looked at Holly. This Jack—this complete stranger—looked as if he understood and cared. She suddenly found herself confessing all the trials of the past three years. All the auditions, the horror-movie part, the thousands of classes. Working as a waitress in an all-night diner because the owner tolerated actresses who had to be on call for auditions.

"No one else knows?" Jack asked when she stopped talking.

"No." And Laurel felt better, though slightly aghast, for having told him. "Adam probably suspects."

Jack chuckled dryly. "Annoying, isn't it? The man's practically psychic."

"You're no slouch yourself."

He smiled. Not a calculated smile, but a real one. "Gutsy and gorgeous. What a package." He stood and held out his hand. "I'm going to enjoy playing with you."

At her expression, Jack's smile widened. "Right after I've had some breakfast."

The man was outrageous, but then again, Laurel had just confessed all her failures while sitting on his luggage in the foyer of her home.

How had he gotten her to do that?

He'd arrived before she'd had coffee, that was how. She always thought better after coffee. If she'd had coffee, she would have thought to ask how he'd managed to get from a rough fishing shack in upstate New York to a Dallas suburb overnight during the most heavily traveled time of the year.

His mother might buy the fishing-shack story, but Laurel didn't. "When did you talk to Adam?"

Jack shoved his hands into fashionably baggy chinos. "A few hours ago."

So the ringing phone hadn't been a dream. "Did he tell you what we wanted?"

Jack took a slow breath, and Laurel knew her questions were beginning to irritate him. "Briefly." The green eyes didn't blink. "Adam Markland said he needed my help. That's all I had to hear."

Embarrassment drowned the rest of her questions. They'd asked him to come and he had. Nothing else should concern her.

She *really* needed that coffee. She offered a smile in silent apology.

He smiled back.

Laurel swallowed and found her throat suddenly dry. Jack was a charmer. "The pot of coffee I started should have finished brewing by now. I'm the only one awake," she added, not certain she wanted to spend too much time alone with him.

"Good. I learn more about a woman at breakfast than at any other meal." He continued smiling. He had perfect teeth.

Laurel quelled the faint flutter in her stomach as she led the way to the kitchen. It was time to dust off her man-managing skills. Anyone as self-assured as Jack would take a lot of managing.

The coffee had brewed, its welcome fragrance permeating the kitchen. Jack headed for the pot, opening cabinets until he found mugs.

"Help yourself," Laurel said with an edge to her voice.

Jack stopped in the act of pouring coffee into his mug and looked at her in surprise. "You on duty or something?"

Laurel blinked twice, then shook her head.

"I don't expect you to wait on me." He reached to the shelf above him and took another mug, filling it with coffee, too. "Here you go."

Laurel accepted the mug, feeling rather petty.

Sipping his coffee, Jack opened the door to the refrigerator. "I heard Texans eat big breakfasts. Eggs! Great." He looked at her. "You like oat bran?"

"No."

"Wonderful. We're going to get along just fine." He pulled out the carton of eggs.

Get along? Laurel felt as if she was being swept along. Better start swimming. "Ever had *huevos rancheros?*" she asked, pulling an iron skillet from beneath the stove.

Jack thought a moment. "Don't think so."

"Good," Laurel said. "Because I've got my own recipe." She pointed toward the refrigerator. "I know there's salsa in there—that red-hot stuff in the jar. How about cheese?"

Jack found both. "I like your recipe already. Butter?"

Laurel nodded. "Or the equivalent."

He brought her the butter dish. Laurel dropped a pat into the heated skillet and listened to the sizzle. "The toaster is in one of the cabinets by the pantry."

"Gotcha."

Laurel heard Jack open and close several drawers after he found the toaster and correctly assumed he was searching for silverware. In a moment, she heard him setting the table. A man who knew his way around the kitchen held a lot of appeal for someone who couldn't function adequately without coffee.

By the time he'd finished and made the toast, Laurel's eggs were ready. "Oh, yeah," Jack said in anticipation as Laurel slid the cheese and salsa-topped mass onto their plates.

They both ate without speaking for several minutes.

"How'd you get here so fast?" Laurel asked.

"Private plane." Jack stood. "More coffee?"

Laurel nodded. "Yours?"

"No. Client owed me a favor."

"And the car?"

"A loaner." Jack shrugged. "Another client. Another favor."

Jack must have powerful clients. But Adam said Jack was no longer with his brokerage firm. And Jack said he'd been holed up in a fishing shack.

So what exactly did Jack do and with what sort of clients?

He tilted his chair back and looked at her. "Go ahead. You're dying to ask."

Laurel was, but she felt considerably miffed that he could read her so easily. No wonder she hadn't been successful as an actress. "Why are you here and not with your family?" she asked, instead.

The two front legs of his chair hit the floor with a thud. "And ignore a distress call from a fraternity brother?"

Laurel shook her head, a disbelieving smile curving her lips. "If *I* got a call from one of my sorority sisters to come and coach her brother at poker—two days before Christmas—I'd think it was a little strange."

"That's 'cause you don't play poker."

"You *said* I could ask."

"But I didn't promise to answer."

Laurel hoped it wasn't necessary to like her poker coach. She opened her mouth to make a cutting remark right back at him when something in his eyes stopped her. There was defiance—and pain. "No, you didn't," she replied, instead. "But... if you were a character I had to study, I'd guess that something happened to you recently and you didn't want to discuss it with your family, so you used us as an excuse to be away over the holidays."

Jack's face was carefully blank, which told her she was correct. "Laurel, my dear, you have the makings of a great poker player."

She felt absurdly pleased.

"You're right, of course," Jack continued, apparently deciding to answer her, after all. "I'm a very, very good stockbroker. Sometimes I make guesses that are on target—the way you did just now. I can make those guesses because I study companies and observe people." Jack's jaw hardened. "Some... less successful brokers have wondered about my amazing luck."

The bitterness in Jack's eyes bothered her, reminding her of her own. "Keep talking. I'm going to unload the dishwasher."

Jack shrugged. "Not much more to say. Do you know what insider trading is?"

"Cheating?"

"Close enough. Also highly illegal. I don't do it." There was a hint of challenge in his voice. Laurel remained silent. "My firm asked me to take a leave of absence while— let me see if I can remember the exact words—'things cooled off.'"

Laurel walked past him, carrying a stack of plates. "So you came here."

"No, I quit and went to a little fishing cabin my family keeps."

"Sounds like you were running away." Laurel bent down to unload pots and pans. When she straightened she saw that Jack was stone-faced.

"In my three years with that firm, I made more money than any other broker. I also lost more money than any broker. I take calculated risks. My clients understand that."

With a flash of insight, Laurel realized that his clients were gamblers, just like Jack. "But the other brokers weren't as understanding, right? Jealousy reared its ugly head, et cetera, et cetera."

"Et cetera." Jack carried their dirty dishes to the sink and rinsed them off while Laurel sorted the clean silverware. "So I quit."

She bumped the drawer shut with her hip. "It's a good thing you can fall back on poker. I suppose I'll have to give Exemplary Temporaries a call." Laurel laughed and pulled out the top rack of the dishwasher. "Unless you're a really great poker teacher."

Jack gripped her arm, and she looked at him in surprise. "Gambling is no way to earn a living."

Laurel stared at him until he released her. "I guess you'd know."

"Yes." His voice was clipped, his face closed. "I don't play anymore."

Obviously, this was a hands-off subject. Maybe some day he'd tell her about it. "Then why are you here? And why did Adam ask you to come?"

"I owed Adam. He doesn't know I gave up cards." Jack's look warned her to keep it that way.

Laurel began unloading glasses. "I can't see you owing anybody for anything."

"It's an old debt." This time, the hand on her arm was gentle. "Sorry."

She watched as he grabbed the sponge and wiped the kitchen table. It was clear that paying back his debts meant a lot to him. She could understand; after all, wasn't that why she'd come back? To repay Holly?

Laurel decided she could like Jack. She no longer thought of him as a shallow man blessed with a model's good looks. Yes, Laurel mused, she could like Jack.

A low whistle pierced her thoughts. "What happened to you?" Standing by the telephone table, Jack studied a framed photograph of Laurel and her sisters at the first charity ball they'd decorated. A considerably more voluptuous Laurel was dressed in a slinky gown of silver lamé. "How long ago was this?"

Laurel lifted a shoulder. "About three years." She turned back to the sink to avoid Jack's scrutiny.

Jack, apparently not one to take a hint, walked over beside her, tilted her chin and held the photograph up to her face. "*Three* years?"

Laurel glared at him.

"A little early for crow's feet, isn't it?" He lowered the photograph. "When you tan, you pay."

On second thought, Laurel decided she was *not* going to like Jack.

"Laurel! I saw the suitcases out in the hall. Did the airline find your luggage?" Holly was inside the kitchen before she noticed Jack.

"You saw Jack's luggage." Laurel introduced him quickly to stifle the speculative gleam in her sister's eyes.

"You're here already? That's great! What do you think of Laurel's poker? Can you help her?"

How like her sister to assume that everyone was as single-minded as she.

Jack shook Holly's outstretched hand. "We haven't played yet. Laurel fed me instead."

"Good idea." Holly said, then frowned as she saw the empty salsa jar.

"Sorry about the hot sauce, Holly."

"No problem. I've got gallons."

Laurel saw Jack hold up the photograph and compare Holly to her younger self.

"Yes, I've put on weight," Holly said, already at the refrigerator. "I'm allowed to put on twenty-five to thirty pounds, according to Ivy's books."

"Not all in the first trimester," Laurel murmured.

"Congratulations, then, I assume." Jack smiled broadly.

"You . . . you didn't think I was just *fat,* did you?" The dismay rang in Holly's voice.

"Oh, no," Jack denied, earning him a beatific smile from Holly, "but painful experience has taught me not to offer congratulations unless the mother-to-be is wearing a shirt with the word 'baby' on it and an arrow pointing south."

Smooth and slick, Laurel thought.

"What did y'all have for breakfast?" Holly scanned the refrigerator for possibilities.

"Huevos rancheros."

Holly straightened and looked at Laurel over the refrigerator door. "That uses hot sauce, right?" she asked thoughtfully.

"Yes." Laurel caught Jack's eyes and had difficulty smothering her smile.

Holly removed the eggs. "Listen, Laurel, I would've offered you clothes, but I thought the airline would find your luggage."

The heat of embarrassment warmed Laurel's cheeks. Her audition dress did look like an odd choice for an early-morning breakfast with a stranger. She involuntarily glanced at Jack, noting his blank expression. A poker face. After her babbling earlier, he would realize she hadn't told Holly she was broke. She hadn't even told Jack exactly how broke she was.

"I can't fit into most of my wardrobe anymore," Holly continued. "You're welcome to borrow anything. Oh, Ivy and I cleared out a bunch of the old clothes we all used to share. We meant to donate them to Goodwill last week, but never got around to it. They're in the cedar closet."

"Thanks." Laurel tried to sound nonchalant. "I'll sort through them and run them by Goodwill for you." She would have liked to set Holly straight about the luggage, but it would be humiliating to do so in front of Jack. "I'll take Jack upstairs, then go through your closet. Like old times."

Holly laughed. "Except this time you've got permission."

Laurel forced a smile and left, murmuring something vague about helping Jack with his luggage.

Her knees shook and she realized how tautly she'd held her body during the conversation with Holly. Holly, who once wouldn't have trusted her to decorate a Christmas tree by herself, had confidence in her now, yet Laurel was worse off than she'd ever been. No hopes, no possessions and no plans.

Reaching the foyer, she slowly sank onto Jack's leather suitcase and had an attack of nerves.

Her family wanted her to be the instrument of their revenge. Granted, it was a rather mild form of revenge, but it was important to them all.

It was especially important, Laurel discovered, to her—for an entirely different reason. She had debts of her own to settle.

She fingered the faded black of her dress. Upstairs, preserved in spicy cedar, were memories, as well as clothes. Knowing Holly, nothing had been discarded. Laurel could slip into clothes she'd once shared as easily as she could slip back into her role as the middle sister who went along with all Holly's plans. But she wasn't the same. And she wouldn't wear those old clothes.

Jack, in all his catalog perfection, strolled toward her, carrying himself with the casual self-confidence success breeds.

One side of his mouth quirked in a knowing grin as he stared down at her. "I used the lost-luggage bit a time or two myself."

It figured. "Only twice?"

"Maybe more." He grabbed the suitcases. "Does that make you a better person, since you've only lied once?"

Her embarrassment before was nothing to the mortification she felt now. "I shouldn't have said that."

"No, you shouldn't have." He let her squirm a moment longer, then his face softened. "Buck up, Laurel. Adversity builds character."

She was loaded with character. Laurel slanted a glance at Jack. He was loaded with character, too.

CHAPTER THREE

HE'D HAVE KNOWN those legs anywhere.

They were encased in denim, but Jack had a warm memory of their tanned length stretching out of a little black dress as the woman who possessed them made the best fried eggs he'd ever eaten.

Jack downshifted the gears on the brand-new candy-apple-red Jaguar he'd bought only moments before. It purred behind Laurel Hall as she struggled along the roadside on high-heeled ostrich-skin boots. He'd offered her a ride home from Goodwill, but she insisted that she'd call a cab. She must have changed her mind. Not that he could blame her; taxis got on his nerves. They were too slow. But they sure beat walking.

The strap of Laurel's purse broke. She stopped, stuffed it into a shopping bag and threw a hank of her off-color hair over her shoulder. The Jag drew level with her as she began walking again.

Jack lowered the window and leaned across the passenger seat. "How about a ride?" He wanted to show off his new car.

Laurel ignored him.

Stifling his impatience, Jack slowed the powerful car to match Laurel's pace.

What was the matter with her? He'd enjoyed her company on the drive over and had thought the feeling was mutual. Then, once they'd arrived at the Goodwill truck in front of the mall, it was obvious that she wanted nothing more to do with him. She could hardly wait for him to leave.

It was a classic brush-off.

What had happened? He replayed bits of their conversation in his mind as Laurel continued to ignore him, and could think of only one reason she wouldn't ride with him. She didn't like speed. It was a shame, too. This little beauty could do zero to sixty in—

A car horn honked behind him and he, in an admittedly adolescent display, floored the accelerator and peeled around Laurel, coming to a stop directly in her path.

She prepared to cross the street.

"Laurel!" He reached over and opened the passenger door. "Get in, will you? I promise I'll drive like we're going to church."

At the sound of her name, Laurel's head jerked toward the red Jag, but she didn't walk closer.

"Laurel, whatever I did or said, I'm sorry." Jack climbed out of the car and slammed the door. "Now will you please come over here and tell me what it is that I'm sorry for?"

"Jack?" Her eyebrows rose inquiringly.

He ripped off his sunglasses. "Who'd you think it was?"

Laurel approached the car and took a slow walk around it. "I didn't know. Wasn't your car blue this morning?"

As realization dawned, Jack smiled sheepishly. "Yeah. Sorry." He helped her stow her shopping bags in the back. "I suppose you get hit on a lot."

"I used to," she said, as they got into the car.

Jack remembered the picture of a voluptuous Laurel in the silver dress and could believe it. Now she didn't even look like the same person. She was thinner, and her hair, no longer Texas blond, hung down her back. She looked much older. And aside from the obvious physical differences, there was a wary disillusionment that lingered in her eyes.

Reaching for the keys, he turned toward her. "Are you mad at me?"

Actress she might be, but she wasn't good enough to fake the startled expression on her face now. "Because you forgot your Jaguar changed color?"

Jack laughed and stared the car. "You like it?" He hoped she did.

She shrugged a shoulder. "What's not to like?"

He'd expected more of a reaction. Then again, he supposed that wasn't really her style. "I enjoyed driving the other car so much, I decided to buy a Jag for myself."

There was a short silence. "What will you do with the car when you return to New York?"

Jack settled comfortably in the leather seat. "I don't think I'll go back to New York."

Laurel raised an eyebrow. The man made major decisions as if he were choosing laundry detergents. A new car. An expensive new car. Immediate travel. Impulsive. Impetuous.

Laurel didn't want impetuous. She wanted stability.

She inhaled the new-car smell. "Is it going to take *that* long to coach me?"

"Depends—" he shot her an oblique look "—on how well we get along."

"We're getting along fine."

"Say that with more enthusiasm."

Laurel suddenly froze, hearing a deeper meaning behind Jack's words. He'd better not try anything with *her*. She wasn't some naive little girl who wouldn't tell on him.

"Just how do you expect to be repaid for your expertise?"

His face screwed up and his jaw sagged. "What?"

If he'd been an actor, she would have said he was overacting. "You want us to be *very* friendly, right?" Bitterness dripped from each word.

Jack pulled into the driveway of her home and drove around to the garage. When he turned to stare at her, he wore a look of genuine shock. "What happened to you in California?"

"*Nothing.*" She waited until his face told her he understood. "Which is why I wasn't given any parts."

Jack tapped his heavy college class ring on the steering wheel. "I thought the old casting-couch cliché was dead."

Laurel shook her head. "Nope."

"Look, lady, I don't take advantage of women that way." The fierce expression on his face reminded Laurel of Adam at his most intimidating.

"I know," Laurel said sarcastically, "because you don't have to." She'd heard that line before.

He leaned very close to her. "That's right," he whispered.

Laurel could see the gold flecks in his pale green eyes. She could smell the rich soap scent that clung to him. She could feel the growing tension in the parked car and knew that she was just plain wrong. Jack wouldn't have to take advantage of women.

"Is that why you snubbed me earlier?"

Laurel shook her head blankly.

"When I dropped you off," Jack clarified.

He was still very close to her. Close enough for her to see that his dark beard would always shadow his face. She wanted to run a finger across it, but wisely refrained.

She moved back a fraction of an inch, uncomfortable with his closeness. He smiled in lazy acknowledgment as he shifted away from her. "What was the problem with me sticking around?"

Her relief quickly turned into embarrassment. Only two of the bags of clothes had gone to Goodwill. The rest she'd sold to the Cardinal resale shop. She cleared her throat. "Honey, I had serious shopping to do. And when a woman's seriously shopping, she doesn't want a man along, unless she's shopping at Tiffany's."

He continued to gaze at her. "And has a man taken you shopping at Tiffany's?"

Laurel gave him a womanly smile. "Yes." She felt an extremely satisfying feminine pleasure at the flash in Jack's eyes. "My father—for my sixteenth birthday."

A corner of his mouth lifted. The money-colored eyes were half-closed. "Then it's been too long."

Laurel's breath caught in her throat. The expensive sports car was suddenly claustrophobic. Jack was still too close. She forced a laugh. "I agree," she said as she felt for the door handle.

She had to get away. Right now. Jack was...bothering her. Laurel couldn't identify her unfamiliar feelings until he winked at her as she slammed the door.

Jack was that rarity, that never-before-encountered unmanageable man.

WHAT NONSENSE. Of course she could manage him. She just needed to restock her ammunition.

Laurel stood in the shower and soaped her hair for the third time. Blond she'd been born, blond she was in her heart and, by golly, blond she'd be again. But when her hair was dry, it still looked as though a storm cloud obscured the sun.

Laurel sorted through the clothes on her bed, grateful to have something to wear other than her jeans and the faded black dress.

As she hung up the clothes from the resale shop, she ripped the black dress off its hanger.

It had been a wonderful dress, but it had served its time. She'd worn the thing to every audition for more than a year. It was now a dark gray, lighter gray under the arms. With accessories, she could be anyone in that dress.

She hated the dress.

It was the symbol of all her failures. But she couldn't unceremoniously throw it away, not after all they'd been through together.

She'd burn it.

Laurel slipped on a red-pants-and-sweater outfit that she'd borrowed from Holly and carried the dress downstairs.

She could hear voices from the front room and from Holly's office, but the den was empty. Laurel lit the logs she found in the fireplace and sat on the floor with her back against the sofa as the flames began to dance. Staring into them, she fingered the limp rayon of the dress, and when the flames were high enough, she blanketed them with it.

There was a whoosh, a few sparks and then Laurel watched her dreams go up in smoke.

"Is that some sort of family tradition?"

Laurel was too depressed to feel embarrassed at being caught by Jack.

He walked over to the fireplace and stared into the fire. "I liked that dress."

Laurel heard the wistful note in his voice and smiled.

"Forget to put it in the Goodwill bag?"

Laurel patted the floor beside her. "Goodwill would have rejected it." She sighed. "That was my audition dress."

Jack grabbed a couple of sofa pillows and handed one to Laurel as he sat next to her. "So now what are you going to do?"

Laurel rested her chin on her knees as she hugged them to her. "Brush up on my poker."

"After that."

"I don't know. I honestly do not know."

There was a short silence. "What do you want to do?"

"I want to be an actress." Out of the corner of her eye, Laurel saw Jack study her.

Slowly he plucked the television guide off the coffee table and tore a small piece of paper from the corner. Rolling the paper into a tiny wad, he threw it into the fire where it burned in a brief, bright blaze. "No, you don't," he pronounced at last.

"I do!"

He shook his head. "You said you wanted to be an actress. You didn't say a word about acting."

Laurel straightened. "What else does an actress do?"

Jack looked as if he was enjoying himself. "Lives the good life, if she's successful. Lots of glamour and attention. Pretty clothes, pretty things."

Sounded good to Laurel. Sounded better than selling and wearing cast-off clothes. "You're accusing me of being shallow and materialistic."

"Aren't you?"

"No, I'm not." Laurel struggled to her feet and glared down at him. "I'm not!"

He grabbed her wrist. "There's nothing wrong with a little materialism."

Her first impulse was to shake off his hand and leave the room immediately. Instead, her eyes narrowed as she mulled over Jack's comment.

How much of their family history did he know? Their huge white-columned house impressed people. She suspected Jack was impressed, too. He would have been a lot more impressed if he'd seen the house before the bankruptcy auction.

Texas bankruptcy laws allowed a man to keep his horse, his homestead and necessary livestock. Translated into modern terms, Laurel and her sisters got to keep the house, some of the land and their car. Furnishings, except for a stated minimum, were put up for auction.

They could have sold the house, but the family owned it outright—as long as they paid the taxes. The three of them had lived in part of the house and used the rest as storage for their Deck the Halls business. Now both Holly and Adam worked out of the grand old place. They had, in the years Laurel had been gone, refurnished many of the rooms. It was good-quality furniture, but not the fine antiques her mother had lovingly collected.

So, it seemed that her brother-in-law's friend made snap judgments on appearances.

Laurel felt her anger grow, its intensity surprising her. She had almost decided to ignore Jack's materialism comment, but couldn't. "You sound like a holdover from the eighties. Wealth is good. Obscene wealth is better. Conspicuous consumption is wonderful."

"Yeah." He grinned a slow, lazy grin.

"You're a horrible person, Jack." Laurel pulled her wrist from his grip.

"And you love it."

"I do not."

"Yes, you do, you just don't want me to know it." He continued to grin, crossing his arms over his chest.

Laurel felt, actually felt, her blood begin to boil. One part of her automatically analyzed the feeling, storing it for future acting reference; the other part simply simmered.

She wanted to commit physical violence.

"Go ahead." Jack still grinned at her.

"What?" She bit off the word.

"You look like you want to take a potshot at me. Here." He reached for the cushion he was sitting on and handed it to her.

Look at that smirk. Obviously he didn't think she'd throw the pillow.

He was wrong.

The pillow connected with a satisfying *whump.*

At first gleeful, then appalled, Laurel braced herself.

"Feel better?" Jack's smile now held more than a bit of self-righteousness as he propped the pillow behind him.

How *dare* he not throw it back at her! Since he'd effectively negated her reason for leaving, Laurel crossed her ankles and sat down again.

"Jack, I—" *Whump.*

The sofa pillow slid all the way down Laurel's body and settled in her lap before she recovered from her surprise. What was she supposed to do now? Criticize him? After she'd belted him with the same pillow?

She glanced up to find him watching her.

He was too attractive for his own good.

And he knew it.

"That wasn't very nice." Laurel allowed a huskiness to melt into her whiskey-pitched voice. It had—used to have—a corresponding effect on men; they melted right along with it.

"Nice is boring." Jack's green eyes reflected a warm gold from the fireplace. He didn't blink. She knew, because she didn't blink, either.

The fire danced and popped and sizzled. Neither Laurel nor Jack moved.

She found herself thinking about Jack and what sort of woman attracted him. Skinny failures with split ends wouldn't interest a man like Jack. But the woman she'd been...

Her breath escaped on a wistful sigh. For the barest fraction of a second, she wished Jack could see her as she'd looked before she'd left for California. She wished with an intensity that brought tears shimmering in her eyes.

Jack propped both hands on the floor, leaned toward her and stopped inches away.

She looked like a miserable waif—she knew she did. The worst of it was that she wanted him to kiss her, but she didn't want him to know it. She gritted her teeth, willing the tears not to fall. Her fingers clawed the corners of the pillow.

Jack's lips curved fractionally.

Laurel's fingers tightened.

Then her body was bending forward, and Jack closed the short distance between them.

It was a soft, gentle, exploratory caress. A pity kiss.

Her tears spilled, dampening his cheeks.

"Hey," he half whispered, half crooned. "Acting means more to you than I realized."

"It's not that," she managed to choke out.

Understanding filled his eyes. Embarrassment filled hers.

"Come here." Jack encircled her with his arms. He murmured soft words against her mouth, then followed them with his lips. The energy radiating from him enveloped them both, reviving Laurel's long-suppressed feelings. Nerve endings deadened by the months of struggling to be an actress suddenly sizzled to life.

A small inner voice tried to tell her that she was revealing a need better left hidden. A louder voice insisted that, at this point, *anyone's* arms would make her body hum.

Laurel ignored both voices and inhaled Jack's soap-scented skin. Her fingers, newly charged, coursed through the cropped layers of hair at the back of his head, pulling him toward her insistently.

She felt his weight shift as one hand caressed her jaw, then stole around to cradle her head, keeping her close as he ended the kiss.

She didn't want the kiss to end. As she drew a shuddering breath, Laurel remembered Jack's telling her that he didn't take advantage of women.

He was right.

And she should be grateful.

Just before he leaned against the sofa again, Laurel reached out and gently ran her fingers over his jaw. She was fascinated by the raspy, yet oddly soft feel of his beard.

"Does my beard bother you?" he asked.

Reminded of where she was—and what she was doing and with whom—Laurel dropped her hand. "No."

Echoing her movement, he crooked a finger and followed the moist trail a tear had left on her cheek. "Were you acting just now?"

Lie! urged one part of her. *Take a chance and tell him the truth,* urged the other.

Laurel took a chance. "No." She watched to see his reaction.

And there it was, that wary look men got when they thought women were about to turn mushy. She braced herself.

And lied. "It was just a kiss, Jack."

His expression warmed. "But a very nice kiss." He grinned. "We'll have to do it again sometime."

Definitely, she thought. "Maybe," she said aloud.

Definitely, she saw in his eyes.

Time to change the subject. She didn't want to experience any more emotional eruptions. Jack made her think and he made her feel. Laurel wasn't ready to do either.

She tried to find a polite way to ask him how he'd become an acknowledged poker expert and when she'd see a demonstration of his expertise—at poker.

But he spoke first. "Other than the acting, how's your life been?"

"Not very well, thank you," Laurel responded, trying to avoid any further deep discussions. "Whoever said 'I've been rich and I've been poor and believe me rich is better' knew the score."

Jack resumed shredding the television guide. "So you headed to California to get rich again."

They were back to money. Hadn't Jack ever heard of small talk? "You are the most exasperating man!"

"Why do you find the truth exasperating?"

"Because it's *your* truth—and it's *not* the truth." Jack had such a way of twisting her thoughts that Laurel wondered if he'd ever studied to be a lawyer. "I tried to be an actress."

"Notice you emphasized being an actress. You never mentioned acting." Another wad of paper hit the fire. "If you'd wanted to act, nothing would have stopped you."

He made it sound so simple. "How about not getting parts? How about not getting paid?"

"Excuses."

The nerve of him! How could he—with his expensive clothes, cars and gadgets insulating him from harsh reality—have accused her of making excuses?

They were darn good excuses, too.

"*Why* does being an actress appeal to you?"

Laurel opened her mouth, then promptly closed it as she realized the awful truth—Jack's truth.

Pretty clothes...attention. Adulation. Fame. Fortune. Especially fortune. Nothing about creating memorable characters.

Could Jack be right?

Her desire to become an actress had arrived relatively late in her life, and only when she and her sisters were struggling to stay afloat financially. Had Laurel mistaken her fantasy of rescuing her sisters with instant fame and wealth for a true calling? *Was* she shallow and materialistic?

"There...might be something in what you say," she said in a stiff-lipped admission.

"Of course there is," Jack assured her. "I may have faults, but being wrong isn't one of them."

Any further thoughts of analyzing her motives vanished, but before she could think of a scathing retort, Jack asked her another question. "What made you choose acting? You could have modeled."

Laurel noted that he spoke in the past tense. "At the time, I was built for comfort, not for speed."

"Yeah." There was a wealth of expression in Jack's voice that left Laurel no doubt he was thinking of her as she appeared in the picture with her sisters. "So now you've got the figure, but you're a bit long in the tooth, right?"

"If you're asking in your own subtle way if I'm a little too old, the answer's yes." Jack didn't surprise her anymore. She could maintain no polite fictions with him.

"So what would Laurel Hall, young woman of means, have done if her circumstances had not been so drastically altered?"

Laurel laughed unwillingly. Jack didn't need any encouragement. "The usual, I suppose. Tried for my Mrs. degree. Become a corporate oil wife. I was ready to join the Junior League, the Symphony League, the Art Guild and a high-visibility disease charity. I guess I didn't want to do anything other than support my husband in whatever wonderful money-making occupation he dreamed up. Become just like my mother."

She stared into the flames. Become just like her mother. She'd never realized it before. "But I do have a business degree, so I thought that a few years after my husband was established, I'd start my own chic little business—you know, designing clothes or jewelry. Selling real estate or interior decorating. All careers with flexible hours so I could still participate in society functions."

Laurel met Jack's steady gaze. "Well, say something. I've given you plenty of material."

"Sounds good to me."

"Maybe that's because you're shallow and materialistic, too." If they were going to examine lives, why not his?

"Maybe." Jack raised his eyebrows and a softer look entered his eyes. "But what man wouldn't want a wife who devoted herself to him?"

Was *that* the type of life she'd described? "I didn't intend to set myself up as a domestic slave."

Jack snapped his fingers. "There's always a catch."

"Have you ever been married?" He certainly wasn't married now. Married men didn't leave their families during Christmas, and they definitely didn't buy Jaguars on a whim.

"Nope."

"Why not?"

"Too busy." Jack threw more paper balls in the fire. Laurel noticed that when she began questioning him, his fingers tore faster and faster.

"Living the good life?"

He looked at her in surprise. "You think I live the good life?"

"Well…" She waved her hands to indicated his clothes. "And the car, new luggage… Yes, I'd say life was good to you."

Jack didn't smile. "Did it occur to you that I might have earned it?" There was an edge to his voice, as if Laurel had accused him of something he found abhorrent.

"Wall Street brokers work hard. Of course you earned it."

Jack's tight look eased. "I did. I worked hard. Very hard." He sighed heavily. "The stuff's new 'cause I just bought it. New York apartments are small. There wasn't room to store luggage. I moved straight from school with cardboard boxes and suitcases I borrowed from my mom. I was always too busy to redecorate or move to a bigger place."

"You bought suitcases just to come here?"

"No." Jack shook his head. "I bought them to move my things to the fishing cabin. I only had suits, so I bought new clothes, too."

A simple, logical explanation. He hadn't gone on a spending spree to impress his old school chum. "Oh," she said, feeling small.

His eyes crinkled at the corners, but he didn't actually smile. "So, after I make you a poker expert, what will you do? Hang around the country club and win all the tournaments?''

''I don't belong to a club,'' Laurel snapped, irritated.

''You're behind schedule.''

''How kind of you to point that out.''

''I'm sorry.'' Jack poked her shoulder as he might have one of his male friends. ''Adam filled me in about Conner Mathison. He says you've played him before.''

Laurel made a dismissive gesture. ''Ages ago, at my father's Wednesday-night poker games.''

''Did you win?''

Laurel smiled in remembrance. Her mother had tacitly looked the other way when her father let her sit in for a few hands. ''Actually, yes, sometimes.''

''They probably let you win,'' Jack said disparagingly.

''I was pretty good,'' Laurel felt compelled to inform him.

''Hmm.'' Jack scanned the den. ''Cards? Chips?''

Laurel pointed to the dark wooden cabinet beside the fireplace. Jack got up and chose a deck of cards, then motioned her to the game table near the leather-topped bar. After repositioning the table to take advantage of the fire's warmth, he held out a chair for her.

''All right, Laurel,'' he said, shuffling quickly and offering her the deck to cut. ''Let's see how good you really are.''

CHAPTER FOUR

"CHEER UP, LAUREL. All you lost was a stack of chips and breakfast in bed." Jack smiled as he watched Laurel fry eggs.

"I don't recall betting on the location." Laurel banged plates on the counter.

Jack hid his smile behind the *Wall Street Journal*. "I like my *huevos rancheros* with lots of cheese."

Laurel made a face at him, which he pretended not to see. "I'm never going to be a card shark," she sighed, slipping his plate in front of him. "I'm more the type who should blow on the dice for good luck."

Jack folded the newspaper. "Yeah, the other guy's dice." At least she realized her limitations.

"Never insult a woman who's holding a pot of hot coffee."

"Or who's related to a lawyer." Jack indicated his mug. "I'm ready for a refill."

Laurel poured it and a cup for herself. "What would you have cooked for me if I'd won?"

"I don't cook. I dial."

She watched as he ate, her own plate untouched. "Was I really that bad, or are you really that good?"

Both, Jack thought, and he was rusty. He wiped his mouth on a napkin. "I've played worse."

"How did it go last night?" Holly trooped into the kitchen, Ivy and Adam right behind her.

Jack, grateful for the interruption, exchanged glances with Adam over Holly's head. Adam lifted an eyebrow ever so slightly. Jack wished he could reassure him. "Laurel does have potential," he began.

"Gee, thanks," Laurel inserted.

"So I'm not ready to fold." One look at the sisters' faces, and he knew he wouldn't be allowed to give up yet, anyway.

"Good." Holly nodded, poured a mug of milk and heated it in the microwave.

Laurel seemed uncertain, giving him the impression that if Holly had said, "Let's quit," Laurel would have agreed without regrets.

"Breakfast looks great," Ivy said, peeping over Laurel's shoulder. "Are you cooking for everybody?"

"Sure." Laurel stood. "Take mine, I haven't eaten any."

Ivy hesitated, and Laurel pushed her into the chair. "Go ahead."

The microwave buzzed and Holly removed her milk, flavoring it with coffee.

Laurel gestured with the iron skillet. "*Huevos rancheros* all around?"

Holly turned slightly green. "I think I'll just have yogurt this morning. I'm not very hungry."

Everyone looked at her in silence, absorbing this radical development. Holly might have blushed, but Jack couldn't tell. The green overpowered any pink tinges.

Adam spoke first, draping an arm around his wife. "I'll join you for a quick yogurt. I've got clients coming in less than half an hour and I want to review the file."

"On Christmas Eve?" Jack asked. He didn't know if he wanted to be left alone with the three sisters. Ivy and Holly influenced Laurel too much. He wondered if she realized it.

"Don't tell me you aren't going to plug your computer into the markets as soon as they open," Adam replied.

Jack grinned. "Money doesn't take a holiday."

"This case concerns child custody over the Christmas holidays," Adam continued. He grabbed two containers of yogurt and handed one to Holly, then got them each a spoon. "We're going to see if we can work something out." He saluted with the spoon and headed out the door.

"So I'm cooking for myself?" Laurel pointed at the egg carton.

"Well..." Jack stared at his plate consideringly.

Laurel took the hint and cracked some more eggs.

"Can you make a poker player out of her in a week?" Holly asked him.

Jack hesitated. Laurel's rigid stance told him his answer was important to her. A week was no time. But if Laurel had the determination he thought she did, anything was possible. "She's going to need lots of practice."

Laurel didn't turn around. She knew she needed practice, but she wasn't sure she wanted to gain it with Jack. She couldn't relax around Jack. He liked to stir things up, and she was ready to settle down and lick her wounds.

As he talked with her sisters, Laurel studied him out of the corner of her eye, pretending he was a character she had to play. She could skim the surface and give a credible portrayal of Jack. But what motivated him? What did he want?

When she asked herself those questions, Laurel realized that Jack's easygoing personality, his outrageous candor, hid the real Jack.

And who was the real Jack? Did he intend to remain an unemployed stockbroker? How was he going to support himself?

Laurel didn't like the direction her thoughts were taking. Jack's personal finances were absolutely none of her business.

"What am I supposed to do when we find Conner?" she said, interrupting Jack's conversation with Holly. "Walk up to him and say, 'Hello, how about a game of high-stakes poker?'"

"We took care of that already," Ivy answered. "I found out that Conner is on the board of directors at the hospital. Money obviously makes a wonderful character reference."

"They're having a fund-raising party," Holly said, scraping the bottom of her yogurt cup. "Naturally they came to me."

"Naturally," Laurel murmured.

Ivy grinned. "She used a casino theme. As a director, Conner will have to attend and he won't be able to resist playing."

She walked over to the telephone table and handed Jack an envelope. "Here's your invitation. You two can see him in action."

"The party's on New Year's Eve." Laurel was reading over Jack's shoulder as she served him more food.

Holly smiled. "Now you'll have a date."

Laurel forced an answering smile, not knowing which was worse—having her sister assume she'd be free on New Year's Eve or actually being free on New Year's Eve. Besides, she had nothing to wear.

"You know—" Jack tapped the invitation "—this is a great idea. Laurel will have a chance to watch Conner and possibly play him. She might—and I emphasize might— wangle an invitation to one of his private games."

"Wonderful." Laurel grimaced, remembering her thorough shellacking at Jack's hands last night.

"Cheer up, Laurel. We've got a whole week." Jack stood and rested his hand briefly on her shoulder. He must have meant the brief physical contact as a gesture of comfort. Laurel didn't feel comforted. She felt doomed.

The doorbell rang. "And another day begins." Holly threw her yogurt carton into the trash and left to answer the door.

"She'll be supervising the packing for the children's wing tonight. Laurel, do you want to help me shop for tomorrow's dinner?" Ivy asked as she carried her dishes over to the sink.

"Still waiting until the last minute?"

"It's more exciting that way, don't you think?"

Jack cleared his throat. "I took the liberty of arranging for Christmas dinner," he announced. "My gift to you all—no dirty dishes to wash."

"Yippee!" Ivy hugged him in gratitude.

What a perfect gift, Laurel thought. Was there such a thing as too perfect? Was she jealous because she couldn't make such a generous gesture? "Jack, it's perfect." Prop up the corners of that smile, she told herself.

"We're usually so busy on Christmas Eve that cooking the holiday meal is more of an endurance test. Now we can watch football all day!" Ivy clasped her hands together.

Christmas Eve. Holly's birthday. Laurel had forgotten, though Ivy's remark about packing for the hospital should have reminded her about their family tradition of decorating the children's wing of the hospital on Holly's birthday. Laurel hadn't even wished her sister a happy birthday. How embarrassing.

"Bye y'all. If I don't have to shop, then I'm off to the newspaper. I'm supposed to observe for a week as prerequisite for a course next semester." Ivy hurried out the back door, leaving Laurel and Jack alone.

Laurel stared at the dirty dishes, thinking how quickly they'd reverted to their old roles. Holly, the breadwinner, Laurel, the cook, and Ivy, the student.

She shrugged and started to load the dishwasher.

"A couple of these books aren't bad." Jack was glancing over the books on poker Ivy had checked out of the library. "I've got to work for a while. Why don't you read this one, and we'll talk about it this afternoon?"

Laurel saw that he held the book on poker strategies. "Do you think reading about how to play will help?"

Jack finished clearing the table. "Knowing how to play poker is only part of the game. There is an…attitude that's necessary to be a winner."

He met her eyes. Without telling her in words, Jack let her know she didn't have that attitude. A winner's attitude. "Don't worry," he said softly, gently tilting her chin with his fingers. "We're going to work on it."

LAUREL THREW DOWN the cards in disgust. "But you *said* never open betting with less than a pair of aces when I'm playing close to the left of the dealer!"

Jack raked in the pot. "You're third to bet, the other two hands dropped and this is a loose game. You could've opened."

"So what's the point of learning all these rules?"

"So you'll know which ones to break."

Laurel shook her head as she moved clockwise one place at the game table.

Jack was dealer and played the five other hands. "I'm trying to teach you to play against type on occasion," he instructed. "Don't let yourself be classed as too conservative, or you won't get any action when you do hold a good hand."

"What about bluffing?"

"Overrated. You shouldn't bluff more than a couple of times in a game, especially if you're caught."

Jack dealt the cards, but Laurel was too discouraged to look at hers.

He glanced at the cards on his left. "Professor Plum folds." He looked at the next hand. "Colonel Mustard checks—what does that tell you, Miss Scarlet?"

Laurel smiled unwillingly. "That Colonel Mustard probably has a medium-high pair and wants to see if anyone has anything better."

"Or?" Jack prompted.

"That Colonel Mustard is sandbagging, trying to increase the amount in the pot by coming back with a raise because he has a strong hand," Laurel recited in a weary voice.

"Or wants you to *think* he has a strong hand."

"In which case, he's bluffing, and I don't know any more than I did!"

"Except that Colonel Mustard isn't swayed by pretty young girls like Miss Scarlet." Jack winked at her.

She tossed her head, Scarlet-style. "How about Mrs. Peacock?"

"Oh, she's always in."

"Of course she is. She tipples and can't think clearly this late in the game." Laurel finally picked up her cards. It was Miss Scarlet's turn. After glancing at her hand, she decided she'd rather be playing Clue after all.

Other than one lonely ace, she had nothing, absolutely nothing. But hadn't Jack just told her to play against type occasionally?

She looked at him. He wore a smirk as he studied Mr. Green's cards.

"I'm in." Laurel tossed a chip into the pot.

Mr. Green promptly called and raised.

Mrs. White dropped. "She has to serve the sandwiches, anyway," Jack explained.

"And you, Mr. Jack of Hearts?"

Jack pretended to study his cards. Laurel knew he made decisions at a glance, so he was trying to intimidate her. His long-fingered hand toyed with a stack of chips, lifting it and letting the chips click back onto the table one by one.

Laurel hated it when he did that and suspected he knew it. She concentrated on acting the part of a poker player.

"The Jack of Hearts sees the call—" a single chip went into the pot "—Mr. Green's raise—" another chip "—and raises." Another chip.

Laurel knew she should drop out; actually she had no business betting in the first place. But it would be just like Jack to bluff at this point.

"Well, what's Colonel Mustard up to?" Laurel asked.

"Alas, Colonel Mustard must drop. However, Mrs. Peacock will throw in two more chips, and you, my dear Miss Scarlet, must as well, unless you wish to fold."

Laurel immediately tossed two chips into the pot.

"Fascinating first round. And now, the draw. Mrs. Peacock will take two. Miss Scarlet?"

Laurel felt her cheeks turn the color of her character. Without meeting Jack's eyes, she asked for four cards, thus revealing that she had nothing of value in her hand. She shouldn't be in this round and she knew it. Now Jack knew it, too. Well, miracles could happen.

One at a time, she drew the cards toward her. No miracle.

"Jack takes one."

One card? Laurel couldn't look at him. She wouldn't be able to tell if he made his hand or not, in any case.

"Mrs. Peacock drops."

It was Laurel's turn.

Jack started clicking the chips again.

She remembered his advice—never bet into a one-card draw. He'd only drawn one card.

"Fold," she sighed, belatedly coming to her senses. "What did you have?" she asked as Jack scraped the chips toward him.

"You didn't pay for the privilege of seeing my cards, Miss Scarlet."

"Come on, Jack." Laurel reached for his cards, and he let her see them.

She stared in disbelief. A queen and garbage. And she'd had an ace! He'd outbluffed her!

Jack looked at her cards. "Too bad." He didn't sound sorry.

"You...!" She pounced on Mrs. Peacock's cards. "You made her drop out when she's got two pairs!"

Jack shrugged. "They were low pairs."

"But you knew you didn't have anything at all!"

"But I won the pot."

"By cheating!"

Jack grabbed her wrist, his eyes hard. "Don't—ever—call—me—a cheat."

She tried to tug her wrist away. Jack didn't seem to notice. "Okay."

He held her wrist a moment longer, then slowly released it.

Laurel glanced down at the white marks as they faded. "You overreacted."

"Did I make my point?"

"Oh, yes." Laurel stood, deliberately regal. She'd leave, but she didn't want to give the impression that she was running away.

"Sit down."

"No."

"I *said* sit down."

"And I *said* no."

By this time, Laurel realized she'd have to back off. She—they—needed Jack. He didn't need them. His position was stronger than hers. Right now, she resented Ivy and Holly almost as much as she resented Jack.

"You didn't say please." She swallowed, hoping Jack would meet her halfway.

He jumped up at once, bowed and pulled out her chair.

"Thank you." Slowly, elegantly, Laurel sank into the leather club chair, not relaxing her muscles until she felt the smooth softness beneath her.

"'Cheat' is not a word you throw around. Understand?"

"I understand that cheaters are—"

He cut her off. "Not so long ago we, or rather your nearest male relative and I, would have been required to meet on a field of honor."

"Men have always been rather touchy about honor."

"Especially gamblers, amateur or otherwise."

Laurel cooled her seething anger. Jack was right, but not in the method he'd used to make his point. On the other hand, she wouldn't forget this lesson. "Would you please explain why you folded Mrs. Peacock when she had two pairs?"

"Each poker game has different personalities. Your job is to define those personalities. You do that very well, possibly because of your acting experience."

Praise from Jack. She tried not to feel flattered.

"Mrs. Peacock chickened out," he concluded.

"Why? I drew four cards, which I realize was stupid, so she knew I didn't have anything!" Laurel pointed out.

Jack hesitated. "Good point. But I only drew one."

"Why?"

"Because it wasn't the traditional move with the kind of hand I held."

"You just wanted to be the one to beat me." Laurel sat back. "I might have held wonderful cards. In fact, if I'd stayed in, I would have beaten you."

Jack shook his head. "You were mad at me. You would've bet on anything. But when you began to think about what you were doing, you lost your nerve."

"I didn't lose my nerve," Laurel insisted through gritted teeth. "I chose not to waste any more chips."

He smiled, and she realized something else. "*That's* why you only drew one card. You'd taught me not to bet against a one-card draw and you were expecting me to remember that."

"Very good. Really."

"I'm so predictable," Laurel said in disgust.

It would've been nice if Jack had denied it, but he didn't.

"You two ready for a break?" Ivy stuck her head in the den.

"I am," Laurel replied. "Time to cook?"

"No!" Ivy frowned, then apologized. "I'm sorry—you don't know. We'll eat turkey with the nurses in the hospital cafeteria. They always have a birthday cake for Holly, too."

Laurel thought of the small one-layer cake she'd baked from scratch that afternoon. She supposed the thought counted, anyway. "I guess we'd better start dressing," Laurel said, including Jack. "I'll bet I can fit into my elf costume."

"I'll bet you can, too, but—" Ivy bit her lip "—Holly can't zip up the Mrs. Claus outfit. She's wearing the stretchy elf tights and shoes with a big red sweater. It doesn't look too bad, but tell Holly she looks great, okay?"

"No Mrs. Claus?"

"We hoped you'd wear that outfit, Laurel."

"Me?" Her mother had been Mrs. Claus for as long as Laurel remembered. When they'd begun decorating the hospital wing again, Holly had worn the costume, and neither Ivy nor Laurel had questioned her right to do so.

Mrs. Claus. At that moment, Laurel realized how much she wanted to wear the outfit. "Okay." Smiling at Ivy, Laurel felt the sting of tears. Crying about it was stupid, and she hoped Jack wouldn't notice. "Jack, do you have a red shirt?"

Jack was playing a game of solitaire. "Nah. I'll stay here and scrounge something to eat for myself."

"You don't want to decorate trees with us?" Ivy looked horrified.

He shook his head.

"C'mon. You'll have fun," Laurel urged, hoping Jack would realize that he was lowering himself in their opinion.

"No."

"It'll make the kids happy." Laurel knew she should drop the subject. Even if he changed his mind now, it would be grudgingly. She remembered how Adam, her brother-in-law, had worn their father's oversize Santa outfit. Of course, he'd been madly in love with Holly at the time. But Laurel wasn't even asking Jack to wear a silly hat.

He contemplated the arrangement of cards. "Not interested."

He was keeping his distance, reminding them that he was here only as a favor to an old friend. He was here to do a job and when he'd done it, he'd leave.

She'd better remember that and make sure she kept her distance, too.

CHAPTER FIVE

HOLLY STARED at the mound of pastel yarn nestled in Christmas wrapping paper. "But I don't know how to knit!"

Laurel waved away Holly's objection. "You'll love knitting. It's just what you need, an activity that lets you sit with your feet propped up and still accomplish something."

She watched as her sister fingered the fuzzy yarn. "A baby's first Christmas tree! I can design knitted ornaments—"

"Holly! That's supposed to be an afghan for *your* baby." But Laurel was too late to prevent her sister from entering a creative fog. She hoped her other gifts—financed with proceeds from the Cardinal resale shop—would be appropriate.

Christmas morning. Everyone was there, surrounded by unopened packages—except Jack, Laurel noted with asperity.

She felt vaguely insulted and nearly apologized to everyone for his absence, though he was Adam's friend. But Adam didn't seem concerned about Jack's antisocial turn, so why was she?

"Where's Jack?" Holly ripped open another present. "I can't wait any longer."

Laurel laughed. "You haven't waited at all."

"Maybe he's asleep." Ivy distributed packages from under the tree.

"He's working at his computer," Adam informed them.

"Not on Christmas morning, he isn't!" Laurel bounded toward the stairs. "What a Scrooge!" She left them laughing, as she'd intended, but she was frustrated by Jack's attitude.

Christmas had always been very important to her family, and she was disappointed that Jack didn't want to join in the festivities. But what could she expect from a man who chose to spend the holiday with strangers rather than his own family?

"Hey, Scrooge!" She stopped outside his room and listened. The door was ajar and she could hear the whirring of a printer. "Jack!" She rapped on the door and peered into the room, expecting to find him characteristically attired in silk pajamas.

He wasn't.

Jack, clad only in a towel and his wristwatch, both hands propped on his hips, stood in front of his computer, his eyes narrowed in concentration. He needed a shave and his damp hair stuck up on one side where a cowlick twirled untamed.

He gave her an unconcerned glance. "Be with you in a sec."

Laurel swallowed, knowing she should leave, but so many emotions bombarded her she couldn't make herself walk away.

She was immediately conscious that she was in a man's bedroom. She was wearing pajamas. He was wearing a towel.

And his entire attention was on a computer screen!

Granted, Laurel thought, looking down at herself, Ivy's gray sweat suit, with an orange University of Texas longhorn emblazoned across the front, was not the stuff of seductions. But she wanted to be pretty. She wanted Jack to think she was pretty.

Tears tightened her throat, angering her. Of all the stupid reasons to wallow in self-pity. Time and life might have faded her looks, but didn't she have more to offer men than her appearance? Couldn't she be desirable anymore?

Just about everyone in California had been attractive, so she'd quickly learned that her beauty no longer gave her an edge.

Now she was no longer attractive.

But Jack was.

His fingers absently combed through his hair as he studied the information appearing on the computer screen. When he reached for the paper rolling out of the printer, Laurel watched the compact muscles ripple across his back. He obviously kept himself in shape but wasn't a fanatic about it.

His waist was trim, his stomach flat. The towel, loosened by his recent movements, began to slip.

Laurel began to sweat in the fleece pajamas.

Jack, his eyes never leaving the monitor, absently tightened the knot in his towel, then suddenly leaned forward and started typing at the keyboard.

Laurel's gaze was riveted on the slice of leg that appeared beneath the parting edges of the towel.

Nice legs. Nice unknobby knees. Terrific thighs...

"How can you even think of working without coffee?" she squeaked.

Jack glanced up with a quick grin. His dark beard made his perfect white teeth even whiter. "Habit. I always think I'll just turn on the computer—warm it up—then I get hooked."

Laurel walked farther into the room, trying for a casualness that matched Jack's. He was treating her as he would a little sister, so she'd better start thinking sisterly thoughts. "What could you possibly find to hook into on Christmas morning?"

"Foreign markets."

Laurel peered at the monitor, but was too far away to read any of the words. "You're missing all the fun."

"Everybody finished downstairs?"

"We're waiting for you."

"*I* have presents?"

He looked at her with astonished delight. He couldn't fake that expression, could he? "Of course," she scoffed.

"Did you buy me a present?"

"No, I—" Laurel broke off her explanation, nonplussed at the flash of disappointment he quickly masked.

"It's okay, I didn't expect you to buy me a present. Unless—" he paused and slowly looked her up and down "—*you're* my present. Shall I close the door?"

"Jack!" She hated the cynicism she heard in his words. He didn't really think she was throwing herself at him, did he? "What I meant was that I didn't *buy* you a present. I had something I thought you'd like."

"A used present."

Laurel sighed. "Antiques might be considered used."

"Is it an antique?" he asked quickly.

"No—"

"Secondhand junk." He shook his head.

"Jack!" Laurel tried to keep the exasperation out of her voice.

"Castoffs."

"No!"

"Oh...I understand. It's the generic Christmas present. The one families wrap and stick under the tree so they aren't caught empty-handed when the neighbor gives them crocheted toilet-tissue covers.''

Laurel started to laugh.

''I'd rather have a Christmas kiss from you.''

Laurel stopped laughing. That wasn't funny or nice or brotherly.

He stood, waiting for her reply. She couldn't think of one.

Instead, she tickled him and ran.

Jack chased her. He could run awfully fast for a man in a towel. Laurel scrambled across the bed, grabbing a pillow to use as a shield.

''Aren't you two a little old for tag?'' Ivy called from the doorway.

''No!'' Laurel and Jack shouted at the same time.

''Will this take long?'' Ivy asked. ''I'm hungry.''

''Oh.'' Jack halted in front of Laurel and checked his watch. ''Don't fix much. The caterers should be here in an hour and they'll bring appetizers.''

His attention was on Ivy, and though it was unfair, Laurel couldn't resist bashing him—not hard—with the pillow.

Slowly, ominously, Jack's head swiveled to face her. Laurel bit her lip. ''Ivy,'' Jack said, his voice deep and purposeful, ''you'd best leave now. You're too young to see this.''

Ivy left, giggling.

Jack advanced toward Laurel. She held the pillow tightly and backed up, step by step, until she felt the edge of the bed against her calves. ''Jack...''

He placed his hands on her unprotected waist.

Laurel squeezed her eyes shut and hunched her shoulders.

His fingers toyed with the hem of her pajama top, flicking it against her ribs.

Laurel could feel the heat from his body and smell the warm, male muskiness.

Her pulse, already pounding from the exercise, quickened. Wait a minute—this was *Jack*. The same Jack who wasn't supposed to affect her.

She felt a push that sent her sprawling on the bed, smothered by the pillow—and Jack.

Warily, she opened her eyes to gaze into his pale green ones. "Do I need to cry uncle?" she asked, casually trying to extricate herself. She didn't want to feel the way she was feeling, which was that it would be nice to be kissed by him. Very nice, but...

"My name is Jack." His voice thickened. "Say my name."

She should stop this right now. Just last night, she'd realized what kind of a person Jack was. An I-don't-want-to-get-involved person.

She stared at the face above her in all its photogenic perfection. The man with the boyish smile. A compelling man. A dangerous man. "Jack," she murmured, unable to stop herself.

One tug and he had removed the pillow between them.

Laurel gasped.

Jack didn't move. He didn't have to.

Laurel could feel his heart beating against hers. He wanted to kiss her, so why didn't he? Just how long did he think she would allow herself to remain in this position? A few wiggles and she'd...

Laurel tried one of those wiggles and froze, acutely aware of what was causing Jack's slow smile. His bare chest pressed against her thin fleece pajama top, under which was nothing but Laurel.

And the knot in his towel was gone.

Her eyes widened, meeting an answering gleam in his.

She drew a deep, shuddering breath—a mistake—and released the air with a whoosh, then attempted to breathe shallowly.

His arms pinned hers to her sides, leaving her hands squeezed against the corded muscles in his thighs.

She tried not to think about all the rest of the places where flesh pressed against fleece.

Tried unsuccessfully.

"May I kiss you?" Jack almost whispered the words.

Of course he could kiss her. "Why do you ask?"

In answer, he lowered his head and nipped at the corner of her mouth.

Laurel immediately inhaled, crushing her breasts against his chest.

Jack groaned and continued his quick kisses, working in words between them. "Because...some women...object...to my beard."

"Fools." Laurel freed her hands, enjoying all the accompanying wiggles, and looped her arms around his neck, drawing him to her.

His beard was a little scratchy, though it looked worse than it felt. She forgot all about his beard as soon as his lips touched hers.

Shocking. Electrifying. Sizzling.

Jiminy Christmas!

How could she allow herself to feel this way? Did she have a choice?

Laurel's hands, buried in Jack's hair, stilled. This wouldn't do. She was about to check into heartbreak hotel with a charming rogue.

Placing her hands under Jack's shoulders, Laurel gently but insistently pushed.

Jack moved his lips about an inch above hers. "Best Christmas kiss I ever had."

"Me, too." She had to give the man his due; it was the best kiss she'd *ever* had. On any holiday. Or any other day. *Or* night.

Gathering the slipping towel, Jack rolled off her. "I know they're waiting for us downstairs, and after your sister's report, they'll be wondering what we're doing."

"Oh—" Laurel struggled to sit up "—I think they'll have a fairly good idea."

Jack ran a finger over her cheek. "I did warn you."

Whisker burn. Laurel felt the sting and blushed.

"That's a good trick. The blush is a close match." He stood and made his way to the bathroom.

"Jack!" Laurel closed her eyes briefly. "Are you always so blunt?"

He returned and handed her a cool, wet washcloth. "If I didn't say anything and you went downstairs, you'd be mad that I didn't tell you about your face."

"Does it look that bad?" Laurel asked as she pressed the cloth to her jaw.

"No." He smiled gently. "You don't know how to look bad."

Her pulse jumped. "To *you* maybe."

"That's right," he said softly. "To me."

Laurel felt tendrils of affection wrap themselves around her heart. Why couldn't she distance herself from this man?

She'd done love scenes in class with absolutely no qualms at all. She should pretend Jack was acting. He probably was.

"Let's see." He tilted her chin from side to side. "Seems fine. Let me get dressed and we'll go open presents!"

As soon as Laurel and Jack walked into the den, Ivy flung her gift at him. "I can't stand waiting any longer. I found the absolute perfect thing. Open my present first."

The laughter, the attention, was focused on Jack, for which Laurel was grateful.

Obligingly, he ripped open the box and silently withdrew two acid-green fuzzy dice.

"For your new car!" Ivy explained helpfully.

"They're..." Jack grappled for the right words.

"Hideous! I know! That's the whole idea," Ivy crowed.

Holly, already knitting, glanced up and shook her head. "Only someone with a car like yours can get away with these."

"Uh..."

"Don't you see? It's the utter perfection of your Jaguar juxtaposed with the...the..." Ivy floundered.

"Atrociousness," Laurel supplied.

"Thank you. Of the green dice." Ivy smiled munificently.

"I see," Jack said, looking as if he wished he didn't.

Adam took pity on him and tossed another present his way.

This time Jack unwrapped a driving cap and leather gloves and looked much relieved.

As everyone tore into their piles of presents, Laurel quietly tugged her gift from under the tree.

Jack unwrapped it slowly and Laurel found herself watching for his reaction.

He didn't rip off the paper the way he had Ivy's, and she hoped he wouldn't be disappointed as he studied the small, gold-embellished box.

"You're right." He grinned his quick, familiar grin. "I should have these."

Why had she expected anything other than his usual reaction?

The plastic crackled as Jack opened gilt-edged playing cards that had been sealed ever since Laurel had bought them at the Schonbrunn Palace in Vienna.

"I remember those cards," Holly said. "You made me stand in the souvenir line for over an hour to buy them."

Laurel shrugged. "I thought they were pretty."

"They're gorgeous." Jack studied the face cards of the deck, which were exquisite representations of the European royalty during the reign of Austria's Maria Theresa. "Are you sure?" He gestured to Laurel with the open pack.

She nodded. "I want you to have them."

"Thanks." For a brief instant, Jack's gaze held hers as he acknowledged her gesture, then he looked away. "Now who did they put on the jack of hearts? That's my special card."

Ha. She'd gotten to him. If she didn't watch it, he'd get to her.

"One last present." Adam scooted an elaborately wrapped box toward Laurel.

Inside, she found a beautiful leather purse. "Thanks, Holly."

"I noticed that the strap on yours was broken."

Laurel maintained her smile. Had Holly also noticed the safety-pin repair?

"Adam picked it out." Holly smiled up at her husband. "He has wonderful taste, doesn't he?"

Laurel murmured appropriately, privately embarrassed—again—by his generosity. She inhaled the rich, warm scent of leather as the doorbell chimed.

"The caterers, I'll bet," Jack said. "Laurel," he said quietly under the cover of rustling wrapping paper. "I'll treasure these. And the thought behind them."

"Don't read anything extra into this, Hartman."

He didn't reply, only sat and looked at her.

A twig of mistletoe landed on the floor between them, compliments of a smirking Ivy. "The caterers want directions."

Ignoring her, Jack leaned forward and kissed Laurel.

"Actually, I meant that for me," Ivy drawled.

Laurel felt uncomfortable. She knew her little sister had spied on her when dates brought her home, but this was different. This was Jack.

He winked as if he knew what she was thinking, then sent a roguish look toward Ivy. "Yeah?"

Ivy now wore the expression of a startled deer. "I was kidding, but not about the caterers."

"Okay." Jack swiftly got to his feet. "I'll be back and we can break in the cards," he said to Laurel.

He was only flirting. She was making too much out of simple flirting. She, as a flirting expert, knew better than to take him seriously.

"Glad you two are getting along so well." Adam squatted beside her.

"We're just kidding around. You know how Jack is." Laurel tried a laugh that didn't quite come off. "This is a beautiful purse," she said quickly, trying to change the subject.

"Look inside," Adam instructed, with a glance over his shoulder. They were alone.

"A matching billfold! Adam." Laurel spoke in a you-shouldn't-have voice. Had they noticed her shabby wallet, too?

"Keep going."

Puzzled, Laurel opened the billfold to find a Neiman-Marcus charge card with her name on it. She kept her head bowed as tears spurted into her eyes.

"You know how to use one of those, I think."

Laurel cleared her throat. "I know that bills do come."

"I put a deposit on your account. If you and Jack plan to move in the same circles as Conner, you'll need new clothes."

Laurel sniffed.

"Think of this as buying costumes for a part you're playing."

She was overwhelmed by Adam's gesture and the faith they all had in her. There had been no resentment, no snide knowing glances, no recriminations. She owed it to her family to help them. "Does Holly know?" Laurel managed to lift her head.

"I didn't tell her." Adam hesitated. "But I have no objection to her knowing."

In other words, Laurel could choose whether or not to tell her sister. She smiled in gratitude. "I guess Holly didn't think of costumes for her leading lady when she planned Conner's downfall."

"She would've eventually realized that you don't have anything to wear on New Year's Eve."

"That sounds fine to me." Jack rejoined them.

Adam stood, nodding to Jack. "After you make a crack like that, I suppose it's my duty to ask your intentions toward my sister-in-law."

"Strictly dishonorable," Jack said immediately.

"Have fun." Adam laughed as he loped down the hall.

Men. They were all alike.

"You have that men-are-such-animals look on your face," Jack commented.

Laurel sighed. He was unnerving.

"How do you feel about your sister's scheme for Conner?" Jack brought out his new pack of cards and began to shuffle.

"I know what she's thinking," Laurel began slowly. "He won on all counts. He destroyed everything. She can't let go of it."

"What's 'it'?"

"Oh—" Laurel ran a hand through her hair "—the helplessness and the frustration. The unfairness. Holly just wants to win once, and then she can put that horrible time behind her."

"I thought the courts had settled everything."

"Legally, yes. Morally, no."

"Are you talking for Holly—or for you?"

She had been talking for Holly, but Laurel realized that she felt the same way. "At the time, it was more Holly's fight, but now I have to do this for me."

"Okay. *That's* the answer I needed." Jack gave her the cards to cut.

"Why?" Laurel asked as she cut three times, the way he'd taught her.

"Because, honey, you've got a lot of work ahead of you." Jack began to deal.

"Think I have a chance? Can I learn enough to beat Conner Mathison?" Suddenly, his answer was very important to her.

Jack picked up his hand of cards. "*We* can beat Conner Mathison."

CHAPTER SIX

LAUREL'S FAVORITE STYLIST at the Neiman-Marcus beauty salon deftly wielded the blow-dryer. Laurel, a small Mona Lisa smile on her lips, watched the results in the mirror.

Gone was the dullness that the dye had left on her dark blond hair. Now her hair, fairest of the three sisters, sparkled with golden lights that had been carefully added by the colorist. Soft waves framed her face in an updated version of the layered style she'd worn in the picture Jack had seen.

She stretched like a cat, her muscles relaxed from the massage she'd treated herself to after arduous hours of shopping. A makeup artist hovered nearby, tubes and jars at the ready. Laurel purred.

She and Jack had been practicing, as they did every day after Jack checked the markets, when Ivy had called from the newspaper. The gossip columnist for one of the big Dallas dailies had phoned in her column. In the ''sightings'' section, she reported that Conner Mathison would be one of a party that evening dining at Black Gold, a popular Dallas restaurant. Jack, seconded by Holly, had immediately suggested he and Laurel plan to be there, as well.

''Think you can doll yourself up enough to attract his attention?'' Jack had asked, the challenge implicit.

''Give me time and a Neiman's card and I can do anything,'' Laurel had drawled in reply.

So Jack had whisked Laurel to Neiman's in his red Jaguar, a fitting chariot for her triumphant return.

Laurel had known exactly the part she was to play tonight and exactly how she wanted to look—flamboyant to the edge of vulgarity, but without crossing the line.

The first dress she'd found was perfect for the New Year's Eve gala. The invitation said to dress in red, black or white, but Laurel had no intention of wearing anything but red.

She needed to stand out and be noticed, and red was a "look at me" color. Her choice had been a long, slim-fitting beaded dress with a high neckline and deeply plunging V in the back. Not many women could wear that dress, and Laurel wouldn't have been able to, either, until recently.

But what about tonight? Black Gold was a trendy night spot, more flashy than formal. Should she find another red dress to ensure that Conner would recognize her on New Year's Eve? The sole purpose of her evening out with Jack was to make an initial contact with Conner so they could casually greet him later that week at the hospital's charity gala.

Tonight was critical. She'd had to choose carefully.

The dress racks had been crammed with the usual black and-gold holiday finery, which Laurel suspected the other women would be wearing. No one dress stood out from any of the others.

And then she'd seen it.

In a niche to the left of the designer evening wear, Laurel found a white angora sweater dress with subdued bugle-bead sparkles. Soft. Approachable. Certainly not something that would be worn by a hard-edged woman bent on revenge.

Laurel had immediately abandoned flamboyant. Holly and Jack wanted pizzazz because that was what they thought Conner would notice. But Laurel knew this dress was better. She'd be a blond snow-bunny among dark winter glitter. She'd look huggable, touchable—yielding.

Now that her hair was finished, it was time to see if she'd chosen the right dress. Laurel stepped into the beauty salon's dressing room, where she removed the plastic protective cape and slithered into the softly clinging dress. She felt sweetly feminine. A final touch-up from the makeup artist and stylist and she'd be ready.

What would Jack think?

JACK SUCKED in his breath, the air hissing between his teeth.

That dress should be outlawed.

Fuzzy white material hugged the tall, honeyed blonde waiting behind the store's glass doorway.

Laurel. A soft Laurel. A gorgeous Laurel. Jack felt his stomach tighten. Conner would have to be blind not to notice Laurel. Jack suddenly felt unreasonably possessive. Protective.

He had underestimated her. He had assumed she would go for eye-catching glitz, but she'd made a far wiser choice. No man would be able to ignore her tonight, and no woman could accuse her of deliberately poaching.

He knew enough about women to know that her luminous makeup and tousled, touchable hair were very carefully created.

Jack drew another deep breath, annoyed by the provocative effect she could have on him without even being aware of his presence. He had just invested a small fortune in tips at Black Gold to see that he and Laurel were seated at the table next to Conner's. He should have saved his money. No man would be unaware of Laurel Hall tonight.

Mesmerized, he walked slowly toward Laurel, oblivious to the chilly evening breeze. He reached the door before she knew he was there.

"Jack!" A swirl of cool air ruffled the hem of the clingy dress.

Though he'd had several minutes to prepare, Jack couldn't think of a worthy verbal offering to the blond goddess before him.

She smiled expectantly, waiting in all her perfection.

His mind was blank.

Her smile faded and uncertainty touched her features.

He wanted to grab her and hold her close, but shoved his hands into his pockets, instead.

"Well, you cleaned up real nice, Jack." Her voice held an inviting drawl.

"Laurel." His voice came out in a hoarse croak. He felt his face flush.

"Is it cold outside? I bought an evening coat, but it's black velvet and I forgot this stuff sheds on everything." She gestured down at herself, and Jack followed each undulating movement of her hand, noting the soft curves, gently outlined but not completely revealed. He remembered the way those curves felt pressed against him and he swallowed.

Say something, his mind ordered.

"WELL, SAY SOMETHING!" Laurel stood, clenching and unclenching her hands. "I thought . . ." Her words trailed off.

Jack was so strangely quiet. Didn't he like the way she looked? Of course he and Holly had told her to go all out, but couldn't he see that taking the subtle approach was better? The beauty of the angora dress was that it was attractive to men and nonthreatening to women.

At least that was what she remembered from her cinema-costumers class. But at Jack's continued silence, the dress that had seemed perfect now seemed insipid.

She'd had the idea that Conner—if he remembered her at all—would think of her as the daughter of his former business partner, the little poker player of more than a decade ago. She didn't want to scare him off this evening; instead, she would be a sweet girl from Conner's past.

And would it be her fault, if his imagination took over?

Laurel watched as Jack struggled to speak, muscles working in his jaw. He was obviously trying to find the words to tell her she looked too juvenile.

He, of course, looked gorgeous. Men weren't supposed to look gorgeous, but Jack couldn't help it. The wind had disarranged his hair, so that strands lay on either side of the off-center cowlick. He casually raked his fingers through it, and it fell into place. Lucky man.

His suit was dark and new, since he hadn't brought any dress clothes to Dallas. The wind had stained his cheeks a ruddy pink, emphasizing the permanent shadow along his jaw.

Laurel wanted to melt into his arms, have him carry her away and forget about scheming to meet Conner Mathison. She'd been anticipating Jack's reaction to her changed appearance all day. She had wanted his pale green eyes to darken with desire. She wanted him to tell her she was beautiful and mean it with his whole heart.

Her self-confidence couldn't survive hearing him tell her she'd chosen wrong, that her instincts had failed her. "I still have the tags. I can exchange this dress for another one." She took a deep breath, noticing that Jack's eyes followed the rise and fall of her chest.

"Don't you dare," he said in a ragged whisper. He stepped closer. "You're a dangerous woman, Laurel." His lips curved in a lazy smile. "And I like dangerous women."

As his words registered, Laurel's poise returned. Had she really struck him speechless? "Yeah? I look okay?"

Then Jack's pale green eyes did darken. "Conner doesn't stand a chance."

That was the whole idea, Laurel thought as they drove to Black Gold. They spent an hour in the bar area waiting for the hostess's signal that Conner's group had arrived, allowing Laurel to make her grand entrance. Would she recognize Conner? Would he recognize her?

"Ready?" Jack touched her elbow and nodded to the hostess. "Break a leg," he whispered.

"I just might in these heels," Laurel muttered.

Her heart beat rapidly, but Laurel walked slowly, gliding between tables and chairs, carefully avoiding eye contact with people in Conner's group.

The hostess paused and waited for them to catch up to her.

Laurel took her time, aware of the surreptitious glances of males watching her progress. When she thought the moment was right, she glanced at Conner's table.

She recognized him at once, an attractive man, his hair silvered but still abundant. He wore a polite smile, outwardly relaxed, but his fingers constantly toyed with silverware, revealing his impatience.

She remembered that about him; he was always crossly impatient, urging others to bet or deal. Turning a friendly poker game into a competition, annoyed when a precocious girl sat in for a few hands. No wonder he'd left her father's game.

If only he'd left her father's company.

She turned her head to murmur to Jack, "The man with the fork." She accompanied her statement with a limpid look for the benefit of anyone who watched. Inside, she seethed.

Jack bent his head as he placed his hand in the small of her back. "I know." His expression told her he understood her feelings.

What were her feelings? How did she feel at this first sight of the man who had ruined her family?

Laurel had expected to feel rage and bitterness. She wasn't prepared for the overwhelming sadness, too. Did Jack sense that?

He removed his hand from her back with a comforting pat.

Show time. The thought renewed Laurel's determination to beat Conner. And to beat him, she had to get his attention. So far, he hadn't noticed her. Time for Plan B.

She went directly to their table, selecting a chair in Conner's line of sight and signaled Jack with her eyes. He responded with a wink and pulled out the chair to seat her. In an exquisitely clumsy move, he tangled the legs of her chair with one at Conner's table.

"I'm so very sorry," he apologized, and flashed a dazzling smile at the woman seated opposite Conner.

She appeared bemused before murmuring a polite, "Not at all."

Conner spoke. "I know you." His statement fell into a puddle of silence as everyone stopped talking to gaze at Jack and Laurel.

Laurel allowed her eyes to meet Conner's, an expression of pretty confusion on her face. "I..."

But Conner wasn't looking at her. He was staring at Jack. Jack regarded him with narrowed eyes, as if he was searching his memory.

Jack wasn't a bad actor, Laurel noted, considering they hadn't discussed a Plan C.

His teeth teased his lower lip and he shook his head slightly, prompting Conner to exclaim, "Vegas. I don't know what year, but we were in a side game together at Binions World Championship of Poker." That was news to Laurel, and apparently news to Jack, as well.

He lifted one shoulder. *Don't overact,* Laurel cautioned silently.

"I never forget a man who beats me at poker," Conner stated.

"Did I?" Jack appeared pleased.

"Yes." Conner nodded and angled his chair toward Jack and Laurel. They still stood by their table, so he waved Jack to the chair closest to his.

It appeared she had needlessly agonized over her choice of a dress.

"Conner?" The woman whose chair Jack had disturbed raised her eyebrows.

Conner had hunkered down, preparing for an extended discussion with Jack. Laurel and his dinner companions might not have existed. "I'm sorry, Patricia." He straightened, masking his irritation.

Laurel felt sorry for Patricia. In fact, if Laurel had been playing herself this evening, she'd have shared Patricia's displeasure.

"This is an old poker buddy of mine."

"Everyone's an old poker buddy of yours," was Patricia's dry response.

"Jack Hartman," Jack inserted, saving Conner the embarrassment of admitting he didn't know his name. "And my companion, Laurel Hall."

Something flickered in Conner's eyes, but it wasn't recognition.

Hall was a common name. Undistinguished. Too bad Jack couldn't have introduced her as Laurel Schnitzenheimer. Conner would have remembered a name like Schnitzenheimer.

Laurel waited for Jack to introduce Conner, then recalled that Jack was pretending not to know Conner.

They'd never get anywhere if Jack kept padding his part like this. "I didn't hear your name," she said, injecting a demureness into her voice she didn't feel. *That's right, Jack, make me seem like a dummy.*

"Conner Mathison."

Conner's expression had warmed somewhat, but Laurel wasn't having the effect she wanted, and he obviously didn't connect her with his former partner.

As she was introduced to the others at the table, she noticed looks of open approval from the men, to which she responded with a sticky sweet smile. This earned her tacit approval from the females.

Conner, however, was more interested in Jack and monopolized him in an awkward conversation between the two tables. If there had been any possible way to squeeze Jack and Laurel in at his table, Laurel was certain Conner would have tried.

Everyone listened with strained politeness as Conner reminisced about past poker games, encouraging Jack to share his stories, too. Jack declined.

Laurel sensed his reluctance to talk poker with Conner, but didn't know if it was because monopolizing the conversation was rude, or because he was troubled by the memories. Jack never wanted to discuss himself, but Laurel would have thought he'd use this opportunity to ingratiate himself with Conner. She smiled to herself. For Jack, *that* would have been acting. He would never try to ingratiate himself with anyone. She doubted he even knew how.

Conner had relaxed from the impatient man he'd been earlier. Jack, on the other hand, began to betray increasing agitation. Somehow she had to find a way to bring the subject around to the hospital's casino party.

"Where do you play these days?" Conner asked, completely oblivious to his silent dinner partners.

Jack included them with a look. "Actually, I'm in town to play for charity." He paused with impeccable timing. "A New Year's Eve casino party."

Very good, Jack, Laurel applauded silently. She listened for a cue. That might have been one, but it would be better if one of the others mentioned that they'd be attending, too.

Patricia did the honors. "For the children's hospital?"

"Yes," Jack affirmed.

"We'll all be there!" Patricia's enthusiasm was probably due to finding a subject of conversation other than poker.

"Not your usual style, is it, Jack?" Conner's voice held a scornful note.

Jack's smile disappeared.

"There's no challenge, is there? Everyone's an amateur."

Laurel couldn't reach Jack to place a warning hand on his arm. She nudged her foot against his calf and saw him swallow before forcing a pleasant expression onto his face. "The idea is to raise money for charity."

"Just what I said—not your usual style." Conner sneered.

Why on earth was he baiting Jack? Laurel hoped Jack wouldn't turn out to be a hothead.

Where was the waitress? She'd be a welcome distraction.

Laurel could feel Jack's anger. His calf muscles tensed. Mentally sighing, she knocked over her water goblet and squealed. Trite, but effective.

She saw Jack smother a smile and hoped he appreciated her diversion. "Ooh. I got your place all wet. I'm sorry, Jack." A lifted eyebrow let her know she'd better cut the Marilyn Monroe breathiness she'd added to her voice.

"I can show you to another table, sir." The busboy, who had instantly materialized, gestured to a secluded corner, which would have been ideal under other circumstances, such as a romantic evening out.

"No, I'll move closer to the lady." Jack did so, his smile back in place.

Laurel assumed that the interruption caused by their flustered waitress and the doggedly efficient busboy would put an end to Conner's gibes.

She was wrong.

"So what's the real story, Hartman? Why're you in town? Big game somewhere?"

Conner was worried about missing some action! Laurel suddenly felt intense sympathy for Patricia. Conner Mathison, with his one-track mind, was a supremely boring man.

Jack reached for his water goblet and Laurel tensed. It would be just like him to spill it. He took a sip, relieving Laurel's apprehension with a tiny wink. "I really am here for the casino party, as a favor to an old friend. His wife is Laurel's sister. She decorates for these society things."

Patricia gasped. "Your sister owns Deck the Halls?"

"Yes." The others gazed at Laurel with new respect. "Yes, she does." Holly would be thrilled when she heard about their reaction.

"You must be very proud of her," Patricia gushed.

"Yes." *Wait a minute.* "I also worked with her until recently." Laurel was aware that she had just dismissed the most difficult two and a half years of her life.

"But you don't now?" Patricia asked, as if it was important to make the distinction.

"No, I moved to California."

"Oh." Patricia shot a look at the other woman. "You're *that* sister."

Laurel involuntarily checked to see if she had a scarlet letter emblazoned on her chest. So her reputation was in shreds. She sneaked a glance at Jack. He gestured toward his water glass and quirked an eyebrow.

See if *she* ever came to his rescue again.

"I didn't realize you knew Doug Hall's girls." Conner ignored Laurel and spoke to Jack.

What was the matter? Couldn't Conner face her? Wasn't she worthy of his notice? Or was he ashamed?

"Laurel's brother-in-law and I are old friends," Jack explained again.

At last Conner turned to her. "I used to see one of you girls when I came to play poker with your daddy."

Laurel smiled and nodded. "Daddy used to let me sit in sometimes." She stared straight at Conner. "I miss him."

Conner stared right back at her. "Yeah. Left our business in a mess."

Left the business in a mess? "You talk like his death was an inconvenience." Laurel struggled to keep her voice under control. The man was as cold-blooded as Holly said he was.

Conner shrugged. "He knew better than to fly a light plane that close to a burning oil well."

"What are you saying?" She was barely aware of anyone else in the room. Until this moment, she'd never understood what drove Holly. She'd had no idea of the injustice and unfairness that her sister had faced as she tried to settle their father's affairs. Laurel had been angry, yes, but the fiery rage she now felt consumed the insulating layer that had shielded her emotions.

"Business was bad. That was one way out." Conner turned to give his orders to the wine steward.

"My mother was in the plane with him." Each word was as distinct as three years of vocal coaching could make it.

She felt Jack's hand take hers under the table and squeeze. It was comforting and cautioning at the same time. Tears threatened. She grasped Jack's hand as hard as she could.

He didn't let go.

"He insisted on flying." Conner shrugged again and shook his head. "I even warned him not to." The others at his table murmured among themselves as the waitress served salads. Conner nodded curtly to Laurel and fixed his attention on his meal.

There had been no remorse in his expression. No quickly hidden fear that Laurel or anyone might suspect he had set the fire. Nothing to indicate that he even remembered what consequences the Hall family had suffered. Had Conner denied what he'd done for so long that he began to believe his own lies?

Laurel drew a shuddering breath. Jack brought their clenched hands to his lips and kissed hers.

She released her grip immediately. "He acts as if he doesn't remember," she choked out.

"Shh." There was a tenderness in Jack's eyes that Laurel hadn't seen before. "You've got to get through the meal," he said so quietly she could barely hear him. "Stay in character."

Stay in character, Laurel repeated over and over to herself. Concentrating on acting a part allowed her to detach her actions from her feelings, as Jack had known it would. "Why didn't you tell me you played Conner before?"

"I didn't know I had."

Laurel reached for her wineglass, admiring the steadiness of her hand. "I want to beat him, Jack." She took a sip of the wine and returned the glass to the table. She glanced once more toward Conner, then gazed at Jack's unsmiling face. "Teach me how."

Jack studied her for a long moment. She'd barter her soul to beat Conner Mathison right now and he couldn't blame her. The dead, defeated look that had been in her eyes when they'd first met was gone and wouldn't return. The desire to beat Conner gave her a new purpose, something to replace her dreams of acting glory for a while.

Jack looked deep into her eyes, reading a defiant plea that went far beyond revenge. He was drawn into the brown depths and knew he'd never be the same. *Teach me,* she'd said.

A corner of his mouth lifted. "Okay."

CHAPTER SEVEN

"DEAL."

"Laurel—"

"Deal."

Jack shrugged and dealt another round of cards. "This last-minute cramming isn't going to help, you know."

Laurel ignored him and studied her cards. "Who's opening?"

"You need experience in an actual game," Jack offered in a quiet voice.

"I'll get plenty of experience tonight. I have to be good enough for Conner to invite me to play after this gala." She looked at her family sitting around the table in the den. "For old times' sake."

Everyone exchanged looks. Laurel was irritated with them. They were worried about her. She'd caught significant looks between Holly and Adam. Between Holly and Jack. Between Ivy and Jack and Holly. Between Jack and Adam. The only people not exchanging significant looks were Jack and herself.

Jack understood. He'd been there when Conner had all but accused her father of committing murder and suicide. The others thought Conner actually believed his own accusations because that was the only way he could live with himself after setting the oil-well fire that had led to his partner's death.

But how did Conner live with himself after embezzling from Laurel's father? Or, for that matter, leaving Laurel and her sisters destitute—forgotten by society—while he still roamed free, regularly appearing in the gossip columns?

How had Holly been able to bear the anger all these years? No wonder Adam had called Laurel home. No wonder he'd tacitly agreed to this scheme. Laurel felt that if she couldn't strike back at Conner, she would burst.

Rage was caustic. Rage was stressful and all-consuming. Rage wasn't healthy, and Laurel knew it. Holly couldn't carry that rage during her pregnancy so Laurel had to take it on.

She inhaled deeply. She'd read about people sustaining corrosive anger for years and letting it rule their lives. She wouldn't have to, because she was going to beat Conner. Maybe not tonight, but sometime.

The hand ended and Laurel raked in the chips with a confident smile. "What do you think?" she asked Jack.

He regarded her through narrowed eyes. "I think you're too cocky."

"Sore loser." She did feel cocky. She had a right to feel cocky.

Jack apparently disagreed. "You aren't that good. No offense to your family, but they aren't challenging players."

"I *am* good!"

Another round of significant looks. Laurel wished they'd stop that.

"You're good here. Try a few games tonight. Who's bankrolling you?"

"What?" Laurel was caught off guard.

"What are you using for betting money?"

"Tonight is for charity!" She looked from Jack to Holly.

Holly, swathed in a loose black dress and a huge fake diamond necklace the others had assured her detracted from her lumpy figure, leaned forward. "Yes, but you still have to buy chips. You just don't get to keep any that you win."

"*What?*"

"Laurel, gambling is illegal in Texas, except for private games among friends."

"Conner has friends?"

Ivy snickered until she saw Holly's stern expression.

"You know what I mean."

"I thought the rules were different for charity," Laurel protested.

"No." Adam and Holly shook their heads in unison, and Jack chuckled.

Laurel felt naive and stupid. "Then why bother?"

Holly explained, "The hospital keeps the money from the chips. Winners exchange their chips for donated prizes. And, hey, there's a mink coat, a new car and a cruise. Also some smaller stuff. Plus, the tickets are five hundred dollars."

Laurel's eyes widened. "You mean this shindig cost us..."

Holly gave her a twisted smile. "Don't worry. We're the hired help."

Laurel sighed.

Holly glanced at Adam's watch and got to her feet. "But the money you'll use for chips is ours."

Laurel sent a stricken look toward Jack.

He snorted in disbelief. "What do you think chips represent?"

How idiotic. Of course she knew, but somehow, using chips wasn't the same as using real money. The responsibility and the trust the others had given her began to weigh heavily.

"I'm your banker," Adam said, smiling reassuringly.

Instead of gratitude, Laurel felt resentment. Adam was always shelling out money for her, as if she were a little kid. He probably paid for Ivy's tuition, too. Ivy worked part-time at an Austin newspaper, but her salary wouldn't be enough to pay college expenses. Adam hadn't just married Holly; he'd married the whole family.

Adam handed Laurel a discreetly folded slip of paper as everyone gathered at the front door. Gentlemanly to the end.

As Jack backed the Jaguar out of the garage, it occurred to Laurel that every article she wore, makeup and hair spray included, had been paid for by her brother-in-law.

He had invested in her, hoping to soothe his wife. Adam was a good man. She didn't want to let him down.

"You're awfully quiet," Jack said. "Opening-night jitters?"

Laurel gazed at the man in the driver's seat. "Everyone's depending on me."

"Yes."

Concentrating on the freeway traffic, Jack didn't add anything more. No platitudes or fortifying pep talks. Laurel could have used some reassurance.

She clicked her nails—very long and very fake—against the pads of her thumbs. Maybe she should have left them the way they were. What if she fumbled a card because of her stupid nails? At the time, she thought they'd make her hands look pretty, and she wanted to look pretty. She thought pretty might distract Conner just a teensy bit. She needed any edge she could get.

"Do you think we're all crazy?" she asked impulsively.

Jack winced and groaned. "Don't ask me that. I was hired to coach you, not to pass judgment."

"*Hired?*" Laurel heard the shrillness in her voice.

"No, no, no." Jack shook his head. "*No.* Poor choice of words."

"That would explain—"

"Explain what?"

Laurel was aware that she was treading in dangerous water. "I've wondered how you can be free to...to take off the way you have."

"We've been over this subject." The set of his jaw warned her that he didn't want it reopened. Tough.

"Shouldn't you be job hunting or something?"

They exited the freeway and stopped at a light on the access road. Jack turned his head to give her a long look. "What's bothering you?"

Laurel hadn't intended to reveal her fear that Jack would return to serious gambling, but since he'd invited her questions... She took a quick breath and blurted out, "Are those stock quotes you read every morning, or...?"

"Or race results?" Bitterness laced his voice. It almost covered up the disillusionment. Almost.

As soon as she heard that tone, Laurel knew she'd made a mistake. She tasted sickening shame as her stomach, already quivering with apprehension, knotted. She'd hurt him by not believing him, by not trusting him, and Jack valued trust.

She could still salvage this, still back off and let them both save face. "No. I wondered if you might be addicted to computer games."

She felt the tension ease. A corner of his mouth tilted as he acknowledged his error.

Only he hadn't made the error. She had. She'd poked into something that wasn't her business and regretted doing so.

Laurel had received the message, loud and clear, that Jack was a solo act. She wouldn't invest emotionally in him. What Jack did with his life was no concern of hers. She didn't care. He could spend his money on cars and clothes, and play computer games all day and gamble all night if he wanted to.

She wasn't going to care.

But she did.

"Not computer games. I've been advising some private clients."

"Oh." *See?* her inner voice mocked.

"Those people were with me long before I joined a firm, and they'll stay with me no matter where I am."

"You sound rather confident." Laurel certainly wasn't. The coming confrontation gnawed on her nerves.

Jack's smile grew. "Tell me, have I impressed you with my dedication to my clients yet?"

"Were you trying to?"

"Sort of."

"Okay. I was impressed."

"Impressed impressed? Or just kind of impressed?"

Laurel chuckled deep in her throat. "I thought you were very conscientious."

"I was shooting for impressed impressed."

"Jack." Laurel laughed again, relieved that he was in his teasing mood. She could handle teasing. "What does it matter?"

"Matter? You people are terribly intimidating."

"We are? My family?"

"Yeah. Adam is..."

"Adam." Laurel supplied with a nod.

"And your sister." Jack shook his head.

"Holly? I know."

"She's an incredible woman."

"I know." Laurel's voice had an edge to it.

"Bugs you, huh?" They were at another stoplight, and Jack turned to watch her face.

Yes, Holly's success bothered her. And Laurel didn't want to be bothered, because Holly deserved her success. She supposed she was horrible for feeling jealous. "Okay, we know Holly and Adam are perfect, but c'mon, Ivy and I..."

"Your little sister is a human computer. You know she memorizes cards?"

"She does?" Laurel hadn't known. "She used to spout sports statistics all the time." Was Jack saying that memorizing cards was an asset? "Maybe she should be playing Conner."

"No," Jack replied without hesitation, then slanted her a look as traffic moved again. "And then there's you."

Laurel sighed, thinking of her recent failure as an actress.

"You're drop-dead gorgeous." Jack stated it as an inarguable fact.

Couldn't he have complimented her with more feeling? "That shouldn't intimidate you. You're gorgeous yourself."

"Yeah?" He sounded so pleased Laurel wished she'd told him he was gorgeous before. A warm sensation drugged the butterflies in her stomach. Laurel felt an urge to touch Jack, which she satisfied by the totally unnecessary act of smoothing a lock of his hair into place.

They arrived at the hotel. Jack handed the teenage attendant his keys and a tip. "I check for mileage and dents, buddy," he warned, watching as the boy drove the car off. "He'll have to impress the girls in somebody else's car."

He turned back to Laurel. "So I'm gorgeous, huh?"

She found his streak of vanity endearing. "Quit fishing, Jack. You know you are. You've got perfect teeth, hair, clothes, manners..." Laurel waved her hand to indicate she could continue.

Jack looked as though he wanted her to. "I thought women liked beefy men. Maybe I should add a few more muscles." He experimented with his biceps.

No. Laurel flushed as memories of his towel-draped figure on Christmas morning made her forget everything else. She liked the sinewy feel of the muscles he already had. They weren't neglected and they weren't overdone. Just right. She drew a steadying breath. She couldn't cope with any more of Jack than there already was. "Some women are rather more refined in their tastes," she said, taking refuge in generalities, rather than letting him know her personal preference.

Jack raised his eyebrows. "Sure. That's what they say, then some guy with a big chest comes along and they melt."

Laurel wanted to leave the subject of Jack's chest. She couldn't believe they were having this conversation, each dressed in evening splendor, walking across the foyer of a once elegant hotel, now winking and blinking like a Las Vegas casino. "Your chest is just fine."

"So's yours." He gave her a Graucho Marx leer and guided her to the ballroom.

They presented their invitation to the woman at the door and were bombarded by the lights and glitz of Holly's decorating at its most uninhibited.

"Wow." Jack stood, hands in the pockets of his tuxedo, and gazed at the glittering brilliance.

Flashing bulbs, buzzers and bells, loud talking and laughter mingled with the clicking of the roulette wheels, the snap of cards and the discreet chink of plastic chips hitting felt-covered tables. The expensive perfumes of a hundred women wafted through the air.

"Wow," Jack said again. "Your sister is one determined woman."

Holly. Always Holly. Laurel was so tired of fighting jealousy. She didn't want to be jealous. She didn't want to resent her sister's success.

"She must think the world of you." Jack's eyes held a new respect.

"What?" How on earth had he reached that conclusion?

Jack gestured with his hand. "She designed you a first-class set because she thought that once Conner saw you, you could reel him in."

"I don't like the way that sounds."

"I don't, either." He offered an apologetic smile. "I meant that she believes once a man sees you, he desires you."

"But that isn't true."

Jack took a step closer. "Isn't it?"

Laurel wanted only one man to desire her, and that man wasn't Conner. At the moment, she didn't care about Conner or anything else except the heated look in Jack's eyes. Her lips parted, but Jack just smiled and led the way to the teller's cage.

Flustered, Laurel tried to compose herself. She had a part to play and Jack knew it.

Blindly shoving the check Adam had given her under the cage opening, Laurel reflected that Jack had done a masterful job of distracting her from the nervousness she felt. She had no doubt that his outrageous bantering and flirting was meant to relax her. She shouldn't read anything into his comments. And letting Laurel see his desire for her was meant to do nothing more than boost her self-confidence.

Grateful, she reached for his hand—the one that wasn't holding a cup of chips—and laced their fingers together.

He smiled down at her, and she was suddenly very glad he was with her.

They posed near the entrance for more than an hour.

"My feet hurt," Laurel breathed while maintaining a pleasant expression.

"Keep telling yourself that those shoes do wonderful things for your legs," Jack whispered.

"Which Conner isn't here to appreciate."

"*I* appreciate them."

"Then you can wear these stupid shoes."

"How about the dress?"

"You know," Laurel mused, "with your build, you'd probably look good in this dress."

"Ouch. You're getting better."

"I learned from the master."

They smiled at each other in perfect understanding.

"Do you think Conner won't show at all?" Ivy asked from behind them.

"Hey, beautiful," Jack said. "Holly let you take a break?"

"Holly doesn't believe in breaks. I'm supposed to ask the guards if they'd like a sandwich."

"I could use a sandwich," Laurel told her.

"Later." Jack took Laurel's elbow and nodded toward the doorway. "Conner's finally arrived. Scram, Ivy. It's show time." He grinned briefly and positioned Laurel with her back to the door. "By the way, have I told you that you have superb taste in clothes?"

"Not in so many words."

"Did you deliberately dress in a color that complements my new car?" Jack was looking at Conner, not at her. Laurel could follow Conner's movement across the room by watching Jack's eyes.

"Have I told you that you have a colossal ego?"

"Not in so many words." He pressed her arm. "Start walking in this direction... Ready? Let loose with that laugh of yours."

Laurel threw her head back and laughed a deep, throaty, attention-grabbing laugh.

"Bingo," Jack whispered.

"Bingo isn't played here tonight." Placing a hand on Jack's arm, Laurel laughed again.

Warning chills prickled up her back, which the deep V of the beaded red dress left bare.

"How's the luck running this evening, Hartman?" Conner, in typical fashion, ignored her.

Laurel turned her head with just enough speed to send her streaked blond hair swirling provocatively around her shoulders. "Hello, Conner."

She'd thought long and hard about what to call him—to his face—deciding that "Mr. Mathison" emphasized their age difference too much. Besides, Jack was only a few years older than she, and he used Conner's first name.

Conner blinked, then let his gaze wander over her with a boldness that bordered on insulting.

Jack slid his arm around her waist, holding her tightly. She could feel his warmth through the scratchy material of the tux and relaxed against him, silently letting him know she liked his possessive gesture. "Laurel and I were just headed to the back to find a little card game."

"I'll join you," Conner said instantly. "Chips?"

Jack pointed out the teller's cage, then urged Laurel toward the area Holly had set up for cards.

"Aren't we waiting for him?" Laurel trotted to keep pace with Jack.

Jack slowed. "Let him come to us."

"What's wrong? Are you angry?"

"You bet I am. I don't care what your plans are. I won't allow him to look at you that way."

Laurel felt wonderful. She loved being the object of Jack's male territorialism. Did he realize he was staking a claim? Did he realize she didn't mind in the least?

Holly hurried toward them. "Is he here? Has he seen you?"

"Yes, and I hope you're happy," Jack grumbled. "He drooled all over your sister."

Holly's gaze flicked from Jack to Laurel and back again. "That was the general idea."

Jack exhaled forcefully. "I don't like it."

"I'm only acting, Jack." Laurel spoke in a soothing voice.

"Yeah, but he isn't."

A thought occurred to Laurel. "Maybe he is."

"What do you mean?" Holly and Jack spoke at the same moment, but Conner found them before Laurel had to answer.

He had practically run across the floor, trailing poor Patricia in his wake. "*Con*ner," she whined.

Why did Patricia put up with him?

"Here, play with these." He thrust a handful of chips at her without even turning around.

Patricia opened her mouth in outrage, but Holly intervened. Leading the miffed woman toward the prize display, Holly threw a good-luck look back over her shoulder.

"What *would* we do without the fairer sex?" Conner smiled a "men only" smile.

The muscles tensed in Jack's jaw.

Laurel appreciated Jack's resentment on her behalf, but now wasn't the time. "I gather Patricia doesn't share your passion for poker?"

Conner shook his silver head.

"I love poker," she said, looking Conner straight in the eye. "I can't imagine living a day without playing it."

Conner stared at her, transparently considering Laurel in a new light. "That's true. You got an early start."

Laurel pretended a keen interest in the game going on at the table nearest them.

"I would have played that hand differently. How about you, Jack?"

"Depends on the circumstances." Jack leaned close to Laurel. "If you'll recall the game with the professor..."

"Which time?" Laurel asked, enjoying her part more and more.

"Tuesday," Jack replied. His lip quivered and Laurel knew he struggled to keep from laughing. All in all, he was doing a pretty good job.

"Yes, of course. How interesting."

"Picked up a few tricks from Jack, have you?" Conner still didn't take her seriously.

"We've played together frequently." Laurel tossed off this piece of information as though it was of no importance.

"I'll just bet you have, sweetie." Conner's gritty laugh scraped Laurel's sensibilities.

She couldn't allow herself to show resentment, and she couldn't allow Jack to, either.

He didn't respond and neither did she. Both kept their gaze, if not their attention, on the game being played in front of them.

"Is she any good?" There was a speculative note in Conner's voice, though he resumed talking to Jack as if Laurel wasn't present. "At poker," he added.

Rather than becoming irritated, Laurel added this offense to the huge list Conner had already compiled, then waited, her heart pounding, for Jack's answer.

"Why don't you find out?" Jack pointed toward a new table being formed by a resourceful Ivy.

"How about a game, Conner?" Laurel urged. "For old times' sake."

He regarded her with barely concealed impatience. "Your daddy won't be here to protect you."

She answered him with a level look. "My daddy hasn't been around to protect me for a long time."

Conner inhaled. "Long ... time."

He gazed at her, and Laurel knew she had transcended being a mere female and become a potential player.

With a curt nod, he sat at the table, granting her an audition.

Laurel sat opposite him, excited that the time had finally come to play against him, but disappointed that Jack hadn't sung her praises. Of course it would have been a strategic error for him to have done so. Still ...

The table filled without Jack. "Aren't you going to play?" Dismay entered Conner's voice.

"Thought you wanted to play with Laurel." Jack shoved his hands into his pockets, spoiling the well-cut lines of his jacket.

Laurel noticed an edge in Jack's tone. Was he nervous for her?

Her breath came quicker. Did that mean Jack doubted her abilities? Would she be able to...

Control. Consciously, Laurel slowed her breathing and wiped her hands on a cocktail napkin.

Conner flashed Laurel a disgruntled look that sent her back through the years. Suddenly it was all right. She'd encountered that look before from Conner. She could almost feel her father's hand on her shoulder telling her to ignore him.

This is for you, Daddy, she thought while she arranged her chips. *And for me.*

She drew a mediocre hand, which didn't particularly bother her. Jack had told her to avoid revealing her conservative playing style this evening. He had cautioned her that if she bet solely on sure hands, no one would raise the betting against her. Though she would minimize her losses by her conservative play, she would minimize her winnings, too. Her overhead—the antes required before each hand—would eat into her profit and she would ultimately come away a loser.

Theoretically, this sounded logical, but every time Laurel threw a chip into the pot, she cringed inside.

Tonight, she had to appear as an appealing player, one who bet liberally. There was a betting limit on each round this evening, and Laurel's strategy was to wangle an invitation to a game with Conner in which there was no limit.

So she shouldn't be feeling much pressure. If she lost by flamboyant play, she'd be welcome in a game for her money. If she won, she'd be welcome for her ability.

On the whole, Laurel would rather have the ability.

And then she won a hand.

Pleasure ripped through her. Laurel concentrated on raking in the chips with a negligence that indicated this was a common occurrence and not the first time in recent memory.

She'd won! Instead of diminishing, the happiness stayed with her. *See, Jack?* She wanted to turn around and display the modest pile of chips.

She imagined his look of approval and basked in it.

She wanted to do it all again. And she did. Two in a row. By winning her second pot, Laurel now had more chips than when she'd started playing.

She could do it. She'd win back the Hall family fortunes. Her self-confidence soared.

She lost the next three hands in a row. To Conner.

Laurel felt a searing disappointment, easily eclipsing her earlier joy.

Conner remained impassive. Laurel hoped her own expression was equally impassive.

Her pile of chips shrank. She had to build them back up. She should take more chances, bet more chips.

She should remember Jack's teaching.

On the next round her hand held promising cards, among them the jack of hearts. Jack's special card. She could hear his voice as he cautioned her that inexperienced players panicked and abandoned their playing method.

Laurel held back with a conservative bet.

And lost.

She experienced black despair. She couldn't win. Everyone depended on her, and she'd let them down.

Barely able to function, Laurel dealt the next hand. She could bet last.

Her excellent betting position didn't help, and neither did the smugness on Conner's face as he gathered more of her dwindling chips.

She passed the cards to the man on her left, the next dealer. She wanted to call time-out and run to Jack for comfort. She wanted him to rub her back and work out the kinks. She wanted him to encourage her.

As the man beside her began to shuffle the cards, a tall, red drink appeared at her right elbow.

Startled, she looked up into Jack's understanding eyes.

He bent down, placed his warm hand at the base of her neck and kneaded the knotted muscles. "Cranberry juice."

Laurel drank, never realizing until that moment how much she liked cranberry juice. The tart sweetness refreshed her. Jack's thoughtfulness exhilarated her.

She smiled at him, catching his quick wink as he took her empty glass.

Sitting straighter in the padded chair, Laurel hesitated before picking up her cards, knowing her hands trembled.

One...two...three queens.

Her heart began to beat rapidly. How could she stand these roller-coaster emotions? Hope, then despair—or elation.

The betting before the draw was quite high, resulting in the largest pot the limit would allow. The largest so far. Obviously, other players thought they had good hands, too.

Now came the draw. Each player discarded a portion of his hand, except Conner. Laurel took two cards and drew two nines.

A full house! Had her luck changed?

A royal flush, which was an ace, king, queen, jack, ten all in one suit, was the best hand, and the odds were astronomically high against someone having it. But a full house was a good, solid hand.

Laurel began to sweat. Not perspire, sweat. She felt rivulets running between her breasts and under her arms. The beaded dress concealed this new display of nervousness, which was one reason she'd chosen it. Performers had long known that beading concealed moisture, and Laurel was no stranger to "flop sweat."

Two other hands could beat hers, a straight flush—five cards of the same suit in sequence—and four of a kind, as well as a higher-ranking full house.

Four players still remained.

Conner didn't pick up his hand again. He leaned back in his chair and fixed Laurel with a steady look and an unwavering smile. Her gaze met his once and he flicked a glance down at her small pile of chips, then back to her face. *This is your last hand,* he seemed to say.

Two players before Conner bet and raised. So did he. It was now Laurel's turn. What should she do? It would cost her all but three of her chips to match the raises.

She forced herself to ignore Conner. He was trying to psych her out and he was succeeding.

Maybe he only held a flush or a straight. Defiantly, she threw in all but three chips. Then added one more. The limit.

The other two players dropped out.

Laurel slowly met Conner's gaze.

His grin widened and he matched her raise.

They stared at each other, Laurel looking deep into the eyes of the man whose obsession with this game had destroyed her father.

She wanted to win this hand. She had to win this hand.

Conner cocked an eyebrow, his mocking grin still in place.

Laurel loathed that grin. There was just one way to get rid of it.

Dredging up a smile of her own, she turned over her cards.

CHAPTER EIGHT

ANNOYINGLY CONFIDENT, Conner flipped over his hand, fanning it out, never glancing at Laurel's cards.

The cards had been exposed for a few seconds, yet still their eyes held, daring each other to be the first to look.

Laurel heard the observers murmur. Mentally she prepared herself. Win or lose, she must act as if this hand were no more important than any other hand. As if losing didn't mean that all the money Adam had given her was gone.

She hadn't even looked at the check. The amount of chips the check bought had been intimidating enough.

The longer she waited, the more attention she drew. Laurel dropped her gaze to the cards spread out on the table.

A roaring filled her ears.

Four twos. Four measly twos.

But they were good enough to beat her lovely full house.

"Too bad, little lady." Dimly, Conner's words registered.

Little lady. Her father's nickname for her. If she allowed herself to, Laurel knew she'd feel ill. Instead, she lifted a shoulder, calling on every bit of her acting ability. There must be no shakiness in her voice, no jerkiness in her movements. "Pity."

A dark form appeared beside her. Jack. Laurel forced herself to smile up at him. "Ready to leave?"

"Nope. Play these." Jack spilled a cup full of red, white and blue chips onto the table in front of her.

"Thought I might get to play you tonight, Hartman." Conner's heavy-lidded eyes watched Laurel stack the chips.

Jack shrugged. "Some other time."

"When?"

Jack seemed bored. "Check with me next week. I'm staying at the Marklands'."

"I'll do that." Conner threw a challenging look at Laurel, which she met with an expression as studiously bored as Jack's.

She quickly tossed a chip into the pot for the ante, and the deal began. She didn't want to play with Jack's chips. What if she lost those, too?

Jack set another glass of cranberry juice beside her. "You're doing fine," he whispered. "I would have played the hand exactly the way you did."

"You would have lost," Laurel whispered back.

"That's right."

His unconcern calmed her as nothing else could have.

When it was her turn to bet, she was ready.

"I WON, I WON, I WON!" Laurel leaned back into the lush padded interior of Jack's car, hugging herself. "Jack, why didn't you tell me winning feels this way?"

"What way is that, Laurel?" Jack's tone sounded flat, as if he wasn't happy for her. Winning was supposed to be the whole point of coaching her in poker strategy—wasn't it?

Laurel inhaled and thought about how to describe the happiness bubbling through her. The thrill almost matched her excitement when she got the part in the sorority horror film and thought she was finally launched in her career.

She felt invincible. At long—very long—last, luck was on her side.

She turned to Jack. "Right now, I feel I can do anything."

Jack nodded slowly.

"Was it like this for you when you played?"

For an endless moment, Laurel thought he wouldn't answer her. "Yes." The word seemed dragged from him. "But strictly speaking, you didn't win all that much."

"Enough for one of the prizes," Laurel protested. What was wrong? "Unless you're referring to the prize I chose."

Jack chuckled. "You aren't planning on throwing a Valentine luncheon decorated by Deck the Halls?"

"No. It was the only way I could give Adam back his chips."

"Which is my point. You, after paying to play in the game, came out even. If you'd been able to cash in your chips, you'd have been left with roughly the same amount of money you had when you started."

"Spoilsport," Laurel teased, still feeling great. Jack's grumbling was normal after the tensions of the evening.

But Jack banged the steering wheel with the flat of his hand. "I expected you to be happy, yes. Pleased, certainly. Confident. *Not* euphoric."

What a grump. Laurel kicked off her shoes and wiggled her toes. "Jealous?"

His lips tightened. "Worried."

"Why?" She hitched up her dress and curled her legs under her so she could rub her feet. "You had enough confidence in me to give me that pile of chips."

"I couldn't let you walk away from the game after that one hand. Conner would never have bothered with you again."

"You mean the only reason he played me was to please you."

"Something like that."

The euphoria faded. "Not because I'm my father's daughter."

"Probably not."

Jack had burst her bubble. Couldn't he have allowed her to hold on to her happiness just a little while longer? It had been so long since she'd been happy. It wasn't fair. She lashed out. "You think you're really hot stuff, don't you?"

Jack turned into her driveway. "Yes. In which way were you referring?"

He was about to embark on another absurd conversation. She refused to indulge him. "Because Conner wants to play you."

"Oh." Jack pressed the remote control for the garage-door opener. "I thought you might be referring to my incredibly attractive and gorgeous self."

"No."

"My chest?"

"Jack." Laurel gritted her teeth. Why wouldn't he be serious? "I don't want to talk about your chest."

"Any other body parts?"

"Yes, your neck. I want to wring it!" Minutes before, she'd been floating. Now she was steaming and he wouldn't even fight with her.

Jack's cheeky grin faded to be replaced by a bleak expression. He parked the car, but neither he nor Laurel opened the doors. They sat in the silvered shadows of the new year.

"How do you feel right now?" He reached out and twirled his finger in a lock of her hair.

She batted his hand away. "Angry."

"Why?"

"Because...because I was so happy and you spoiled it!"

"You were *too* happy."

She stared at him. Now he was serious! "Too happy? I've worked hard. I won tonight. I deserve a little happiness."

"Your toes tingled, huh?"

"Yes!"

Jack leaned toward her. "There are other ways to make your toes tingle."

At the unmistakable look in his eyes, Laurel's heart beat faster. He was about to kiss her and she, weak female that she was, was going to let him. She'd probably kiss him back, too.

Why was he doing this to her? He never acted the way he was supposed to. And that kept her from acting the way *she* was supposed to.

He confused and amused her. Exasperated her, encouraged her and supported her. He refused to be categorized. She'd never known anyone like him.

She sighed, yielding.

Jack's lips met hers, gentle and seeking.

She was most definitely going to kiss him back. But none of this tender stuff. She hooked her hands around his neck and pulled him closer. For an instant, he responded; then, with a tiny sound, he pulled away.

"Your skin is so soft." He ran light fingers down her cheek and around to the back of her neck.

Laurel shivered. "Yours isn't." Her thumb traced the roughness of his beard.

"I know."

Laurel's hand stilled. "But let's not worry about your beard," she whispered, drawing his head toward hers.

He more than met her halfway, taking her mouth in a kiss. Laurel felt tingles, dangerous tingles, that weren't due to Jack's beard. In fact, she forgot all about his beard as one of his hands slipped under her velvet cloak and caressed the bare skin of her back.

Laurel's spine arched in reaction, bringing her even closer to Jack, enveloping her in his warmth.

"This dress has been driving me insane. I've been standing behind you for hours, dreaming of touching your back. I know every freckle, but could only imagine how your skin felt."

Laurel nuzzled the side of his neck while his words poured over her in a sensual stream.

"Your skin is softer than the velvet," Jack whispered before kissing her again.

A sweet yearning ache spread through her, surprising Laurel with its intensity. Kisses and pretty words had never affected her this way. Jack had never affected her this way, but the combination of the two provoked a powerful, elemental response.

She didn't want him to leave. Ever.

"Are your toes tingling yet?" He smiled and gently touched her lips.

"Mmm." They were. Her toes were tingling.

"See? This is just as good as winning."

"Different," Laurel said, resting her head against his chest. Jack's heart thundered in her ear. She smiled, not only pleased, but satisfied with herself. "We make a great team." *We should stick together,* she thought, but didn't dare say.

"You were wonderful tonight. Your inexperience never showed."

"I must be a natural," she murmured.

Jack stiffened. "You were also lucky." The pounding of his heart belied the lightness of his tone.

"People make their own luck." Laurel pulled out of Jack's arms. "But I do feel lucky." Surely he must know how she felt. Hadn't he ever felt like this?

As the warm glow of their heated kisses cooled, Laurel felt the euphoria of her win return.

"You do understand that you had to pay real money for those chips, don't you?" Jack reminded her.

"Yes, Jack," she said in a singsong.

"And you played for several hours—"

"And still had all my chips!" she crowed triumphantly.

The air in the car turned even cooler, as did Jack's expression. The silence was filled with the distant pops of firecrackers welcoming the new year.

"Only because I gave you more after you lost them all." Regret sounded in his voice.

And he thought *she* was the conservative player. "Which just tells me I should have started with more chips. My luck changed on the very next hand!" It was so simple, this poker.

"You could have lost."

"I'm too good to lose. In fact, after we clean out Conner, I think we should make the rounds. I could make a living at this." Laurel had been kidding, but Jack obviously took her remarks seriously.

"What have I done?" he asked in a barely audible whisper. Jerking open the car door, he stalked around to her side and yanked open her door, too. "Get out."

"Not until—"

Jack seized her arm and nearly dragged her out of his car. He slammed the door and steered her roughly toward the house.

"Don't even *think* of becoming a professional gambler."

Laurel hadn't actually considered any such thing, but she wasn't about to be ordered around by Jack. One minute, he'd said passionately beautiful things to her; the next, he thought he had the right to determine her life. He didn't, not yet, anyway, and maybe he never would.

"If I want to become a professional gambler, it's my business, not yours!" Laurel closed the kitchen door with a bang.

"Don't you understand?" He raked the fingers of one hand through his hair, which fell on either side of the cowlick, then loosened his tie. "Those men probably let you win a few times."

"They did not!"

"I'd bet on it." Jack nodded vigorously.

"Why? And don't tell me it was for charity."

"You're pretty. They enjoyed your company and some of them probably remembered your parents. You'd leave if you ran out of chips, so they saw to it that you didn't run out of chips for a while."

"No!" Laurel backed away from him. She didn't know this Jack. She didn't want to know this Jack. "I'm good. You said I was good!"

Jack advanced, shaking his head. "I'll show you how good you are." He jerked an arm toward the den. "Start with any amount of chips you want. No-limit betting. I'll clean you out in two hours."

Fury paralyzed Laurel. Either she was good or she wasn't. If she wasn't, she'd better find out now.

And if she wasn't any good, then Jack had been lying all along.

As she stalked into the den, Laurel blinked back tears of outrage. She would *not* let him make her cry. Not ever.

Had teaching her been just another game to him? She dumped the entire box of chips onto the felt-covered table and gestured for him to take some.

His face expressionless—a poker face, Laurel told herself—Jack counted out a third of the chips.

Laurel drew deep gulping breaths. How insulting! She stacked the rest of the chips, trying for a poker face of her own, and mentally divided them. She'd play with exactly the amount Jack had taken. She'd never touch the rest. She wouldn't need to, because she was going to win and win big.

She'd show him how good he was as a teacher. Tossing her hair defiantly, she sat down, reached for the cards first and began to shuffle.

Jack stood, hands shoved into his pockets and stared at her.

She shuffled three times, the slap of the cards the only sound in the room. Squaring the deck, Laurel risked a glance up at him and indicated that it was time for him to cut the cards.

He looked at her, the poker face slipping. Deep within the money-colored eyes, Laurel thought she saw sadness.

Well, he'd started it.

She glanced at the cards and raised her eyebrows.

Jack inhaled slowly and reached down, tapping the deck with one manicured finger, signaling that he declined the cut.

He'd told her never to do that. Startled, she studied his face for an explanation. They hadn't begun to play and he'd already broken one of his own rules.

The first whisper of doubt raised gooseflesh on her skin. She fumbled the cards slightly, intensely annoyed with herself for doing so.

Still silent, Jack sat in the chair opposite her, watching as she dealt.

Just before Laurel picked up her cards, she looked at Jack.

There was a softness to his mouth, but not to his eyes. They were as hard as pale jade. Without looking at the cards he'd been dealt, he took ten blue chips and tossed them into the corner of the table.

The gesture rattled Laurel, even though she knew it was meant to. In this game, white chips represented one unit, or one dollar, reds, five dollars, and blues, ten dollars. Right off, Jack had bet chips representing one hundred dollars—and amounting to a pot bigger than any in the charity game.

She felt her heart beating. Her palms were damp, and she couldn't even wipe them on her dress, because of the beading. She fumbled with her chips, refusing to look at her cards, either. It didn't matter what they were; she had to match Jack's bet or lose the hand.

He probably expected her to throw in extra chips to prove she could play as loosely as he.

Well, forget it. He might abandon common sense, but she wouldn't. That was probably what he wanted her to do, anyway. She'd show him. Clean her out in two hours, would he? Ha!

Four hands later, Laurel had to dip into the chips she swore she wouldn't touch. Half a dozen hands after that, Jack looked at her, then at the chips she had left and pushed an equal number of his own to the center of the table.

She had to match the bet or drop.

She bit her lip, denuded of lipstick long ago. Resentment began to build. Jack had played wildly and irrationally, making huge bets and intimidating her. He hadn't spoken a word since they'd started. He'd broken rules he'd drummed into her. She'd then tried to break the same rules and had suffered the consequences—she'd lost, and he hadn't been fooled. It was almost as if he could see her cards, but she knew he couldn't.

She stared at him and he stared back. Her cards hadn't been spectacular. Right now, she had two pairs. The way Jack had been playing, he could have anything from a royal flush to garbage.

Laurel almost let him take the pot, hoping for better cards the next hand.

But wasn't that precisely what he'd expect her to do? Wasn't that what he'd taught her to do?

Laurel gathered her fraying confidence and pushed all her chips to the center of the table where they mingled with Jack's precisely arranged stacks.

He immediately flipped over his cards. Three jacks, including, ironically enough, the jack of hearts. "It's my lucky card," he said, speaking for the first time.

The clock chimed twice. He'd won in less than an hour.

Laurel threw her cards at him. "How could you do that?" She knocked over her chair as she stood up. "*Why* did you do that?"

Jack didn't move.

Laurel's voice grew louder. "Answer me!"

Jack bowed his head.

Laurel picked up two handfuls of chips and threw those, too. Why wouldn't he speak? Say "I told you so"? Gloat?

His silence infuriated her. With a strangled cry, she scattered chips and cards all over the floor, like a two-year-old having a tantrum.

She was behaving badly and she knew it. "Why?"

"How do you feel right now?" He shot the question at her.

"I hate you!" she shrieked, her voice cracking as she lost what little control she had left.

He'd made her lose control. He'd made her cry. She hadn't cried in California, not once. She hated him for making her cry.

She covered her face and sobbed.

Two strong arms enveloped her in a familiar warmth. For a brief instant, she yielded to the solace Jack offered, then she balled her fists and beat them against his chest until great gulping sobs overcame her.

He still held her shaking body close. She could feel the vibrations as he murmured soothing but unintelligible words.

How could he be noble when she was acting so horribly? She'd screamed her hate at him without effect.

"It's all right," he crooned.

"I—hate you," she hiccuped.

"I know." He swayed from side to side, comforting her as he might have comforted a child, waiting until the storm passed.

"People were laughing at me tonight, weren't they?"

"No one was laughing at you."

"They...they played with me as if I was still a little girl."

She felt, rather than heard, his quiet chuckle. "*Nobody* thought you were a little girl."

"You know what I mean." A leftover sob caught in her voice.

Jack sighed. "They weren't the kind of players you'll find in a no-limit game like Conner plays in."

Laurel pushed herself out of Jack's arms. She didn't want to be held by *him* ever again. "Will I find players like *you*?"

"Yes," Jack said without apology.

"That was what this little demonstration was all about, right? Let Laurel see how the big boys play?"

"You were talking about becoming a professional gambler. The stack of chips you lost just now represented thousands of dollars. How do you feel about that?"

Laurel involuntarily glanced at the chip-strewn floor. "You keep talking about my feelings."

"Because you were elated, exhilarated...intoxicated with the joy of being a winner." Jack took a deep breath. "Then you were hysterical when I burst your bubble. That's not normal behavior, Laurel."

Laurel stooped down and began picking up chips. "I don't suppose it occurred to you that part of my joy might have been from playing—and holding my own—against Conner? That I felt I had a chance to beat him later? That, for once, my sister could depend on me and I wouldn't let her down?"

Jack squatted on the floor next to her. "You needed to know how to handle losing—what your reactions would be." He stood and trickled chips onto the table. "Now you know."

Laurel was still too angry to be embarrassed by her uncivilized behavior. "I felt betrayed. You broke all the rules."

"Those are poker strategies, not rules. Conner will have a different set. I wanted you to know how losing felt."

"Thanks a lot." Laurel tossed chips and cards on the table.

"So...tell me how you feel."

Laurel shot him a furious look to let him know she wasn't about to discuss her feelings.

"Okay, I'll tell you," he said, then moved quickly to stand in front of her. "You feel sick to your stomach. You had all that money and it went so quickly. You kept thinking your luck would change with one more hand."

Laurel stepped around him, but he blocked her way, forcing her to stay and listen. "Or maybe you think you should've changed your style of playing. But the game is over now, so you put it down to a run of bad luck and wonder where your next pile of chips is coming from, who'll lend you money."

Laurel tried to shut out his words. She determinedly gathered chips and cards, concentrating on the ones that had landed in the far corners of the room.

But Jack's words followed her. "Soon you'll start thinking about the next game. You're impatient because you've got to take time to sleep and eat when all you want to do is regain that on-top-of-the-world feeling. Am I right?"

She didn't have to be a psychological genius to know that Jack spoke from experience. Her stomach did feel sick, but it *was* after two in the morning. She hadn't eaten in hours. She'd been under tremendous emotional stress. And of course she wanted to win; who in their right mind would want to lose? "I scarcely think I'm as obsessed as that," she said.

Jack shoved his hands into his pockets. "Oh, you've got all the symptoms."

"Not to worry—I don't have any money."

"That never stopped me."

Laurel sorted through the chips. "Is this where I get the lecture on the depraved depths to which hard-core gamblers sink?"

"It wouldn't hurt." Jack leaned his hip against the table.

She lifted one beaded shoulder. "Then come on into the kitchen. Depravity always gives me an appetite." She was out of the room before he could protest.

Jack caught up with her at the refrigerator. "Great," Laurel said, staring into its cold depths. "Holly's gone nutritious on us. Yogurt or salad?"

"Laurel—"

"Or look. Yummy, yummy sprouts."

"Laurel—"

"What's in here?"

"Laur—"

"Oh, my God!" Her hands covered her mouth.

"What is it?" Jack gripped her arms.

"Liver."

Now she'd done it. Jack's hands tightened fractionally before he whirled her around and slammed the refrigerator door shut with his foot.

In the silence that followed, Laurel heard two tiny pings as a bead or two escaped from her atrociously expensive dress and bounced on the kitchen floor.

She was back in Jack's arms not ten minutes after she'd vowed never to be there again. Funny how these things happened.

"Laurel?" Jack waited, but she decided not to interrupt. She also decided to stay in his arms.

"I did not come here with the intention of coaching you to become a professional gambler."

"And I have no intention of becoming one."

Jack looked skeptical. "But you should have seen yourself. You loved winning."

She didn't want to discuss that anymore. She wanted to discuss the hold her estimable brother-in-law had on this quicksilver man. "What did you owe Adam?"

"You think you're changing the subject." A corner of his mouth lifted. "One semester, the night before spring registration, I gambled away my tuition money. Adam was one of a group of frat brothers who chipped in so I could register the next morning. They used money that was supposed to be a deposit on a room and a band for the Valentine's Day dance."

"What happened?"

Jack sighed. "I couldn't pay them back in time and they had to cancel the dance. I tried to borrow money from every relative and friend I could think of. They'd already lent me money I hadn't paid back. And I'd sold my car, my watch. My books."

"Your textbooks?" Laurel pulled back far enough to look at him, but he wouldn't—or couldn't—meet her eyes.

"Yeah, and I still gambled. The night the dance was supposed to be held, I was in a game."

"I'm surprised they didn't kick you out of the fraternity."

"They did. They were going to sue me, too. But some of the seniors, including Adam, thought I'd learned my lesson."

"And had you?" Laurel slipped the question in. The answer was terribly important. It would help her understand the man she was very much afraid she was falling in love with.

Falling in love with Jack. What a stupid thing to do.

CHAPTER NINE

FALL IN LOVE with Jack? *Jack?* Jack wasn't husband material.

Husbands were stable and dependable, maybe even a little dull. But that was what Laurel wanted. She'd had her adventures. She wanted to settle down.

How could she have let this happen? Couldn't she have kept love out of their relationship?

Just how bad was it? Was Jack a reformed rogue or merely a rogue? "Did you learn your lesson?" she repeated, shaking him slightly.

He hesitated, and the longer he did, the more nervous Laurel became. Maybe she didn't want to hear his answer, after all. "Yes and no," he said finally.

What kind of answer was that? Laurel searched his face. "Are you saying you still gamble?"

Jack heard the tremor in her voice. Of course he still gambled. Everyone gambled at one time or another. But he knew that wasn't what she meant. She meant poker.

She meant late nights in smoke-filled rooms. She meant red-eyed men in need of a shower and shave, playing out of haunted desperation.

He almost smiled as he visualized every gambling cliché in literature and movies occurring to her. "No," he answered. "No, I don't gamble anymore." And he never intended to again.

Her face softened in relief, telling him more than he suspected she wanted to tell him. She cared for him. Knowing that she cared made it easier to talk about a part of his life of which he was not particularly proud.

"There's more, isn't there?"

Jack struggled to find the words to explain without disgusting her. "I still *want* to gamble. I'll always want to. But I never will again. When I realized that gambling controlled me rather than me controlling it, I quit. Now I fight the desire. Do you understand, Laurel?"

She nodded, but he knew she didn't really.

"I remember that feeling you had earlier. That invincible feeling. It's addictive. This evening, I wanted to join you at the table. I almost did. Didn't you wonder why I had chips? But I fought—and won. I stared at your magnificent back and promised myself I'd touch it only if I stayed away from that game." His mouth tilted in a wry grin. "It's been torture—of more than one kind—teaching you poker tactics."

Jack felt drained. Reluctantly he released her, then slowly sat down at the kitchen table.

He could see that she was shocked. But why not? It was a shocking confession, admitting his private demons. Admitting that what was a pleasant entertainment for some had become his obsession.

Laurel was strong, independent, determined. She wouldn't tolerate weakness. But, oh, how he wished she'd understand.

Laurel pressed shaking fingers to her forehead. "Then how could Adam ask you to come here? That's like asking someone who's on a diet to... to judge a chocolate-éclair bake-off."

Jack raised an eyebrow. "Maybe not *exactly* the same."

"You know what I mean." She sat at the table with him, her expression concerned but not disgusted.

Encouraged, Jack risked a comment. "Adam has no idea how bad it was. Only someone who suffers from a compulsion would understand." He paused, hoping she'd realize he wanted *her* to understand. "And we've been out of touch since he moved. He doesn't know I gave up poker years ago."

Laurel blinked rapidly, her eyes bright. Were those tears? "And you didn't tell him, did you?"

Jack shook his head.

"That was very foolish, but very brave," she said on a sigh.

He didn't want her to turn him into some kind of hero! "Not brave. I owed Adam, that's all."

Laurel sniffed. "You've been..." She reached into the drawer behind her and grabbed a tissue.

Oh, no. "Hey, don't cry. I hate it when women cry."

Laurel dabbed her eyes in a pretty gesture. "You're an honorable man, Jack."

"Yeah, compared to Conner."

"Compared to anyone." Admiration shone in her face.

Now she'd put him on a pedestal. He had to jump off and fast. "Don't make me into someone I'm not," he warned.

"You've got integrity. I admire that."

Jack shook his head again. This was not going well. He was turning into her white knight when all he wanted to do was deglamorize gambling and gamblers, make her wary.

In fact, after watching Conner in action tonight, Jack disliked the whole idea of Laurel's going anywhere near the man. "If I'm so honorable, then I've got no business letting you associate with Conner."

"Why not?"

He'd anticipated her question, but he hesitated to answer. Rumors had swirled around Conner years ago. Jack had even heard a few whispers this evening, but then, he'd been listening for any talk about Conner.

On Christmas Eve, Jack had phoned some of his old Texas contacts to investigate the man Laurel and her sisters were so upset about. Without openly accusing Conner of anything, Jack's former associates had let him know that Conner wasn't welcome in their games. Another interesting tidbit was that no women played in any of Conner's games.

He eyed her speculatively. Her square jaw was set, warning him she'd insist on a thorough answer.

Well, she wasn't a child.

"Conner probably cheats," he said baldly.

"Wouldn't surprise me."

"He . . . finds it difficult to locate people to play with."

"Am I supposed to feel *sorry* for him?"

"No." She was supposed to reconsider playing him. "I don't think he likes women."

"I figured that out. Look at the way he treats that woman, Patricia." Laurel's eyes narrowed. "What's your point?"

Jack leaned forward. "The point is that if you play Conner, he won't feel bound by any rules of fair play."

"Surprise, surprise." Laurel laughed. "In other words, if he's going to cheat, it'll be against me, an unimportant female."

"Yes." She should be nervous. *He* was nervous.

"Good." Laurel rubbed her hands together, as if readying for battle. "We can expose him."

"No." Jack spoke sharply, concerned for Laurel and her family. No, he *definitely* didn't want her around Conner anymore. He wished she and her sisters would forget their plan.

Laurel's hands thudded to the table. "Why not?"

"Too dangerous." How could he explain what being exposed might do to a man like Conner? "You don't want Conner as an enemy."

Laurel began to laugh. "How could it be worse than when he was a friend?"

"Oh, Laurel." Jack sighed, then reached across the table and took her hands in his, willing her to understand.

"Is this the obligatory disclaimer you give all your students?" She smiled. "Don't worry. I no longer have any inflated opinions about my poker ability."

"You're not that bad."

Laurel grimaced. "Just not that great."

"You need some seasoning."

"Well? Aren't you going to teach me those dirty tricks you demonstrated so expertly?"

The more they talked, the more uneasy Jack became. She was still determined to see this game through and thought he had a magic formula for making her a winner. "I watched the way Conner looked at you tonight. With contempt. I don't know whether he feels it for you as a woman, as your father's daughter or as a poker player. And you don't need to find out."

"Jack." Laurel squeezed his hands. "I'll be okay. You'll be there with me. Won't you?"

He heard the uncertainty in her voice. She thought he was about to abandon her.

Maybe that would be for the best.

He studied her. She trusted him. She was convinced that he guaranteed her victory. Jack felt a heavy weight settle on his shoulders. What if she lost?

He released her hands and closed his eyes. "It's late." He thought for a few moments. The only way Laurel would stop trying for a confrontation with Conner was if her family decided they wanted to give up. That was it. Laurel would not willingly refuse to play Conner, because that would let her family down. The decision to quit must come from them. "Tomorrow, we need to have a family discussion."

DID HE REALIZE he'd said "family"? Laurel wondered as she sat at the kitchen table the next afternoon. The remains of lunch crowded the kitchen counter. Ivy, who had loudly proclaimed her desire to watch a football game on TV, pouted. Holly and Jack argued. Adam looked worried.

And Laurel daydreamed. Family. He'd said family. Did that mean Jack subconsciously considered himself one of the family? Was he planning to stay after her victory over Conner?

What a wonderful man Jack was, she mused, conveniently pushing all former uncertainties about him into a small corner of her heart. Heroic. Honorable. Decent.

Available.

He hadn't told her he loved her yet, but he would. He was probably waiting until the situation with Conner was resolved.

Or maybe Jack didn't know he loved her yet, but she'd seen love in his eyes. And, last night, for the first time, he'd carried on a conversation without teasing her. A serious conversation. He'd revealed his vulnerable side. Men didn't do that unless they were falling in love.

Laurel felt a thrill of anticipation. She hoped the game with Conner would be soon.

"Why are you smiling?" The harsh tone in Holly's voice jerked Laurel's attention back to the discussion. "Haven't you been listening to what Jack said? He thinks we should forget everything. Give up! Let Conner get away with his cheating."

Before Laurel could reply, the phone rang.

"That's probably Conner." Jack sighed. "Shall I answer?"

At Adam's nod, he cleared his throat, picked up the receiver and spoke. After listening a moment, he signaled that Conner was the caller.

"Looks like we'll have to make a decision soon," Adam said.

"Well, hey, I'll go along with whatever you all decide," Ivy said, edging toward the door. "I'll be in the den watching TV."

"What do you think?" Holly asked Laurel. "It's up to you. Want to go through with our plan or not?"

How could they ask her to decide? If she said no, Holly would be disappointed in her. If she said no, Jack would leave. "The sooner the better."

"Jack has doubts."

"He's being overprotective." Laurel glanced at Jack.

He hung up the phone and sat down at the table again. Laurel reached for his hand and laced her fingers through his. He gave her a quick, tight smile.

"Conner invited me to a game starting at four o'clock." He squeezed Laurel's hand, then disentangled his fingers.

She felt rejected, but told herself she shouldn't. This was business. "Today?"

Jack nodded.

"What did you tell him?"

Jack looked at her, obviously weighing his words. "I told him *we* were playing elsewhere." He waited for her reaction.

"Are we?"

"You up to it?"

Laurel smiled. He cared. "Of course."

"Okay." Jack tapped the edge of the table with his fingers, apparently deciding Laurel and her family knew the risks in associating with bad-guy Conner. "I know of a game tonight. Gentle players, older couples. An excellent start for you."

"Start?" Laurel questioned. "What do you consider last night?"

"The atmosphere was completely different at the party." Jack glanced at Holly and Adam. "There will be no limit to the betting in this game. You need practice playing for high stakes."

Laurel felt her face flush. "Talk to Adam and Holly. They're the bankers." She stood, not wanting to hear the discussion that was sure to follow—a discussion of Laurel's chances and of how much money to give her. She knew they'd talk more freely without her there. "I'll be watching TV with Ivy. She loves to explain the plays to people."

Ivy's play-by-play discussion of football games on two channels washed over Laurel. What was Jack saying about her? He certainly wasn't full of confidence, was he? He was worried. He was concerned.

Great. How was she supposed to play with any assurance, especially after last night's demonstration?

"Yes!" Ivy, completely engrossed in the television, jumped up. "Did you see that pass? First and goal inside the five!"

Right now, Laurel felt as if it was fourth down deep in her own territory and her quarterback was waffling.

"Touchdown!" Ivy yelled a few seconds later.

If only everything could be that simple.

BUT POKER WASN'T SIMPLE. Nothing was simple.

In the dim predawn after the game, Laurel stretched full-length on the den sofa and stared at the beams in the ceiling.

Gentle people, ha! If ever there was an illustration of wolves in sheep's clothing, it had been the expensively clad but ruthless players she'd just encountered.

She hadn't spoken to Jack on the interminable drive home. She hadn't been able to. She had been aware of his glances, his concern, but what Laurel couldn't figure out was whether Jack truly thought these people were gentle—such a deceptive word—or if he was still trying to scare her.

Okay, she was scared. So scared she hadn't slept a wink. She might never sleep again.

She groaned and covered her eyes with the crook of her elbow. She'd lost. Big-time.

All that money. Enough money to pay the rent on her shabby apartment in Los Angeles for months—if she still lived there. Enough for weeks of acting classes—if she still wanted them.

Enough to finance a new start here in Dallas. Gone. All gone in a few hours of play.

Laurel didn't know what to think, and she'd had plenty of hours to think during the long night she'd just spent.

Had Jack set her up? If he had, then how could she have misjudged him? How could she have thought herself in love with him?

"What are you doing in here?" Jack's voice. Concerned.

"Watching TV."

"It's more interesting if you turn the set on."

"I like it better this way." She slid her arm down from her eyes.

Jack walked into her line of sight and nudged her feet. Laurel pulled them out of the way and he sat down.

"I made some coffee." He set a steaming mug on the stack of magazines in front of her.

Laurel sniffed in the faint aroma, then raised herself to peer into the mug. She could see clear to the bottom. "You call that coffee?"

"I don't make it very often."

"I can see why."

"Can't we just give me some points for the thought?"

"Yeah," Laurel said, with a morose look. "You need points."

Jack sighed. "About last night—"

Laurel's short burst of laughter interrupted him. "That line usually comes after activity other than a poker game."

Jack regarded her steadily, his eyes unreadable. "It's my fault. I've been out of touch too long." At her silence he asked, "Aren't you going to contradict me?"

"Nope. It *is* your fault."

"I've played with one of the men before. He's a courtly Southern gentleman. Or was."

"Was. Definitely was. There weren't any hothouse Southern belles there, either. *I* shouldn't have been there." Laurel moaned, and buried her face in her hands. "How can I tell Adam and Holly that I lost all their money?"

"They knew there weren't any guarantees."

"You don't sound very sympathetic. It'll take me years to pay them back."

Jack ran his hands through his hair, then reached for her coffee and took a sip. He grimaced and set the mug down on the magazines again. "They don't expect you to pay them back. This is a joint project."

"But I'm the one who lost the money." She'd mentally replayed hands in excruciating detail all night long.

"Sometimes that happens."

Laurel sat up. "I've got losing down pat now, Jack."

He smiled without humor. "I was trying to boost your confidence."

"Confidence?" Laurel slammed her fist into a sofa pillow. "I don't have any left to boost! I know why I lost. I was too conservative, wasn't I?"

"Maybe on a few—"

"I panicked. I just panicked. My hands shook, I felt sick to my stomach, my mind went blank, I took wild risks when I shouldn't. Everything you warned me not to do, I did. I knew it was wrong and I did it, anyway."

She bent her head over the pillow and felt Jack tuck a lock of her hair behind her ear. "You must be really angry with me," he whispered.

"No," she said into the pillow. "I feel kind of numb."

"That'll pass. Remember what they say about horses?"

"Don't you dare compare this to falling off a horse and getting right back on again."

"It's exactly the same." He planted a chaste kiss on her temple. "I'm going to make a few phone calls while you eat breakfast."

"I'm not hungry." Laurel refused to budge from the sofa. "And no more games. My poker-playing days are over."

Jack stood and pulled her to her feet. "This will be a practice game. Just for chips. No pressure."

Laurel shook her head and tried to twist out of his grasp. "I don't think so...."

Jack pushed her toward the kitchen. "Just play this one game. Then decide whether you want to play Conner, or not."

LAUREL COULDN'T BELIEVE Jack had actually talked her into another poker game only hours after the last fiasco.

And she couldn't believe she was actually winning. It figured. When she played for chips, she won. When it really counted, she lost.

She stacked a tall column of blue chips and tossed them into the pot. Her eye caught Jack's stern expression warning her that she was being reckless.

Oh, piffle. She was enjoying herself. It was just a practice game, for heaven's sake, and Jack wasn't playing.

She won the hand, unable to suppress the smug I-told-you-so smile on her face.

"Hang on," said a player identified to her only as Slim. "I need more chips."

Laurel stretched her arms and legs as the players took a short break. How about that. She was in the middle of a poker game with a guy named Slim. All she needed now was a saloon-girl outfit.

How sweet of Jack to find her such charming men to practice with. He must have told them about her confidence-shattering experience. He apparently knew them from "the old days."

There were four older men, and they called her "ma'am" and "little lady" the way her father had. She didn't mind. They amused her with tall poker tales, and all in all, Laurel was sorry when the time allotted to the game ended.

"Cleaned me out, little lady," Slim said, scraping his few remaining chips off the table.

"Thanks." She smiled at them. "I...I know Jack probably told you what happened to me last night and how awful I felt, and I appreciate what you've done."

"You should," snorted Slim, gesturing to the healthy pile of chips in front of Laurel.

"Oh." She dismissed the chips with a wave. "I know the game wasn't very exciting for you, but I do appreciate your taking the time to play just for fun."

Slim had flipped a cigarette lighter open and stopped in the act of lighting his cigarette. The flame danced, but the men were still.

She saw four pairs of eyes glance at Jack, then at each other, and—with a sinking sensation that was becoming more and more familiar to her—she understood. "I think these chips are worth a little more than I thought, aren't they?" She stared at Jack.

"Depends on what you consider playing for fun stakes, ma'am," one of the men answered.

This was horrible. Laurel felt the blood drain from her face. "Jack...who paid for my chips?"

Grinning, Jack shoved both hands into his pockets. "I did."

He was very obviously pleased with himself. Laurel didn't know what to think. She didn't know what to feel, other than stunned. She didn't know how much the chips were worth, but from the elaborately casual attitudes of the men, it must be a bundle.

She had to get out of here before reaction set in. "Why, thanks, Jack," she drawled with less than her usual aplomb. The men watched them closely.

"Been bankrolled a time or two myself," Slim offered. "But not always with your results." He finished lighting his cigarette with a snap of the lighter. "Interesting, Jack."

"Didn't want her to lose her nerve."

"Some say *you* lost your nerve."

Jack's grin didn't waver. "What do you think?"

Slim cleared his throat with a hacking cough. "I think I'd like another crack at winning my money back."

"I'm getting a little game together for Friday. You're all invited."

"Just us?"

"Thought I'd also ask Conner Mathison—you know him?"

Laurel sat quietly, realizing what Jack was up to. He was setting up her game with Conner. She noticed the unenthusiastic expressions on the men's faces and was afraid they'd refuse.

"Ah, Jack, you don't want her to play with him."

"He and the...little lady here have some unfinished business."

Smiles of anticipation lit the men's faces. "In that case..."

Laurel waited until they were in the car pulling away from the apartment building before she pounced on Jack. "Y-you...you..."

"You're sputtering."

"You—I could have lost!"

"But you didn't." He grinned.

It was hard to stay angry when he looked so delighted. Her anger faded. He must believe in her, after all. "Just tell me—did I win enough to pay back Holly and Adam?"

"Oh, yeah."

"Oh, no." Laurel moaned. "Don't ever tell me how much money was involved. I don't want to know."

Jack regarded her with an amused look. "This is a refreshing twist, feeling horrible after winning."

"I'm not cut out for gambling."

"Good. Give it up after the next game. Because, Laurel—" he paused until she looked at him "—I want your word that, win or lose, you'll quit trying to play poker with Conner."

"Just with Conner?"

"I'm serious." The grin was gone.

"But I might not win." Maybe he was too confident in her.

"He's bad news, Laurel."

"Jack—"

"Promise me," he insisted.

Laurel stared at his unsmiling face. "You're piling pressure on me. That means I've only got one chance to beat him."

"I want your word, or I call the guys and tell them the game's off."

"Okay," she snapped. "Okay. I don't like it, but okay."

She could feel her stomach already tightening with nerves.

Friday was it. The big showdown.

Something else occurred to her. After the game, his debt to Adam would be paid in full. There wouldn't be any reason for Jack to remain in Dallas. And she'd just given her word that this would be her only attempt to beat Conner at poker.

So, Friday night, win or lose, it was over. Jack could go home on Saturday. Alone.

Would he?

CHAPTER TEN

LAUREL WAS a nervous wreck by the time Friday arrived.

She'd been pepped by Holly, warned by Adam, informed by Ivy and coached by Jack. They'd all advised her to relax and have fun. Then they'd given her tight little smiles—which told her they had no intention of following their own advice—and said it didn't matter if she won or lost.

Ha.

And not only that, Jack had distanced himself from her. No cozy cuddling, intimate conversations or intimate anything.

Laurel knew her concentration should be focused on Conner and the game, but she couldn't stop thinking about Jack.

Several times Conner had phoned expressing his eagerness to play those sweet men she'd met the other day.

Only they weren't sweet men. Apparently Slim, whose full name was Slim Richardson, B. J. Brown, E. Lane Scott and Mac Andrews were well-known, high-stakes poker players. They owned car dealerships in Texas—Slim had sold Jack the Jag—and played together when they could.

Laurel shivered whenever she thought of her game with them. She alternated between being pleased that Jack must indeed believe in her abilities, and outraged that he hadn't told her she was playing for vast amounts of money.

"It's just a question of attitude," he'd said when she'd asked him.

She'd had attitude then, but she didn't now.

And Jack's attitude remained a complete mystery to her. Would he simply say goodbye and leave? Was he going to ignore his feelings?

For that matter, what were his feelings?

She sat at the kitchen table, spooned yogurt directly from the container and tried to swallow. She wanted food she didn't have to chew.

"I'm glad you're trying to eat." Jack wandered into the kitchen, smiled briefly and grabbed a carton of yogurt for himself. "Mind if I join you?"

Laurel shook her head. *Ask him his plans. Don't give him a chance to leave this kitchen without telling you how he feels.* "I like yogurt with the fruit on the bottom," she said. "How about you?" *Way to go, Laurel.*

"Prestirred." He beat the yogurt with a spoon, frowning at the lumps.

That's it. We're incompatible. Laurel stared at her yogurt. Suddenly it was too cold and too sweet.

"I don't suppose you feel like whipping up a batch of *huevos rancheros,* do you?"

Her stomach lurched. "In the middle of the afternoon?"

Jack shrugged.

"I'll make them for breakfast tomorrow—or Sunday." Laurel watched his face as he scooped around the yogurty lumps.

"Okay." Jack stopped stirring his yogurt. "I guess I'm not hungry, after all." He sighed, setting the plastic carton on the counter, then made his way out of the kitchen.

He had done absolutely nothing for her peace of mind. Now she couldn't even force down the yogurt. Her hands were clammy, and her stomach was queasy.

This was worse than any audition.

Laurel shivered. Abandoning her yogurt, she wandered into the den.

Jack was repositioning the game table and chairs. Holly and Adam were arguing. Ivy stood, holding a video camera.

"We could attach it to that beam—" Holly pointed to the den ceiling "—and they'd just think it was a security camera."

"The battery pack would wear out after an hour, Holly," Adam said with infinite patience. Laurel smiled to herself. Adam was so wary of Holly's emotional storms that he used his bland lawyer tone with her all the time.

"What's this about?" Laurel asked Ivy.

"Holly wants to tape the game so she can savor the victory. Those are her words." Ivy rolled her eyes.

"I think I'm going to be sick." Or she might scream. Either way, she had to do something. She settled for a walk outside.

Her family was driving her crazy. This was a battle campaign planned in excruciating detail. They'd spent days discussing what they should wear. What they should be doing during the actual game. Where Jack should be. Where Laurel should sit. Where the table should be positioned. When the breaks would occur and what snacks would be available.

They wouldn't let Laurel concern herself. Every time she walked into a room during one of their planning sessions, they shooed her out and told her to rest and eat protein.

Jack had acted the same way. Practicing wasn't fun anymore. He drilled Laurel on pot odds, hand odds and likely betting situations. He never teased her; he rarely smiled.

But he'd stare at her, and she couldn't tell what he was thinking.

Laurel stopped walking and took a deep breath, exhaling a white cloud into the crisp afternoon. Time to turn back. Time to prepare herself. Time to confront Conner so she could get on with her future.

JACK FELT QUEASY. Already dressed for the coming confrontation, he sat at the game table and tested the various positions, while everyone else got on each other's nerves.

Laurel had played an inspired game against the car salesmen, but Jack had no illusions about today. Today was cutthroat time. Each of those men had played Conner before, and none had enjoyed the experience. Laurel was bound to get caught in the cross fire.

Jack sighed. He hoped she wouldn't hate him. He'd tried to make her aware of all the risks. She'd won—and she'd lost. And she'd promised not to play Conner again after today.

Looking at her sisters, Jack wondered if Laurel would be able to keep her promise after he left.

He *was* leaving, wasn't he?

Jack piled packs of unopened cards on top of each other, then knocked them over.

There was no reason for him to stay on after the game, but the thought of leaving depressed him. If he was honest with himself, he'd admit it was the thought of leaving Laurel that depressed him.

If he was honest with himself, he'd admit he wanted to take her with him.

A door slammed, and a rosy-cheeked Laurel appeared in the doorway of the den and flashed him one of her heart-stopping smiles.

Jack felt the corners of his mouth turn up in response. She looked glorious, like an ancient Viking princess ready to do battle.

Something deep inside Jack responded. His pulse quickened. His breathing quickened. He felt his body prepare to fight along with her.

And for her.

They had to talk, and the sooner the better.

But Laurel glanced at her sisters and Adam, still grousing among themselves, put a finger to her lips, then wiggled her fingers in farewell and continued down the hall.

Damn this game, anyway.

CONNER'S FULL HEAD of silver hair glinted in the carefully placed lighting as he scraped his winnings toward him.

Ivy, Jack, Holly and Adam pretended a superficial interest in the proceedings, but Laurel knew they'd just seen her lose her best hand of the evening.

Losing no longer surprised Laurel, but losing this particular hand had. It was almost as if Conner knew what cards she held.

Involuntarily, her disbelieving gaze met Slim's dark eyes. Something flickered in them, and he gestured for an unopened deck of cards.

Laurel hadn't been idle in the days preceding this game. Jack had taught her how to calculate the odds so she'd know whether to risk a bet, and how she could make reasonable guesses about the other players' hands. She'd blown it this time, but took some comfort from the fact that she hadn't been the only loser this round.

"Break," announced B.J.

Conner favored him with the slow glance that meant, Laurel had learned, he was extremely annoyed.

She was ready for a break. She felt her lack of experience keenly and the game was a strain. Calculating pot odds didn't come automatically for her, and she found herself using more math than she had since college.

Thinking furiously while appearing to be casually unconcerned added to the stress.

She looked for Jack and saw him talking with some of the others. Ivy, bless her, chattered as she served sandwiches. She'd called one of her journalism professors and convinced him that poker was a sport and that she had a rare opportunity for some interviews. He'd agreed to accept her stories, so Ivy was getting a head start on her next semester's work.

Laurel was glad someone was profiting from this evening.

"You girls don't like me very much, do you?" Conner's gravelly voice grated on her nerves.

Fortunately, Laurel was watching Jack and the others and had a chance to compose her face.

"You resent the fact that I'm here and your daddy isn't."

Laurel raised an eyebrow and turned toward Conner.

The gall of the man! How could he bring up her father out of the blue like that?

And then she understood. Conner was trying to upset her, to affect her play. But she was emotionally drained. Numb. She'd get angry later.

She stared at him, gradually allowing contempt to show on her face.

His own expression remained impassive. "I warned him not to fly out to that well."

"Did you?" Laurel's voice was calm. She felt powerful right then. Anger—temporarily burned-out—wasn't controlling her. Anxiety had dissipated.

A muscle jumped in Conner's cheek. "What are you implying?"

Now Laurel's other eyebrow lifted, changing her expression to one of ingenuousness.

At her silence, Conner reddened. "I know you and your sisters think I did your daddy wrong. And I know you told the attorney general."

"And you know he decided we were...mistaken." Her smile was as Mona Lisa-like as she could make it.

"And if you're anything like your father, you don't believe him," Conner said, his gruff voice nearly a whisper.

What a great exit line he'd given her. Laurel decided to use it. She pushed her chair back from the table and got to her feet. "I *am* my father's daughter."

She turned and walked quickly toward the sandwich tray. Gliding was out. One couldn't glide on quivery knees.

Halfway across the room, she felt light-headed. Black ringed her vision, but Laurel willed herself to keep walking. She would not stumble in front of Conner.

A blurry figure separated itself from the group near the sandwiches and grasped her by the arms.

"Steady," Jack whispered. "Your face is all white. What did he say to you?"

"Tried to psych me out." She grinned. "Didn't work."

"Hmm." Jack steered her toward the food. "Slim thinks you should have won that last hand."

Laurel bit into the best roast-beef sandwich she'd ever tasted. "So do I."

"Do me a favor and watch Conner when he deals."

Laurel stopped chewing and her eyes widened. "What am I looking for?"

"You can't..." Jack inhaled slowly. "Watch his hands, watch the cards you get, but don't *do* anything."

They thought Conner was cheating! She swallowed, then reached for a glass of iced tea. "Any proof?"

Jack barely shook his head, his demeanor letting her know of Conner's approach.

Conner brushed past, nodded to Holly, who was bringing in a plate of cookies, and made courtly remarks to Ivy. Ivy blushed and looked acutely uncomfortable. Hate radiated from Holly's eyes. No wonder Laurel was the one chosen to play Conner. Her sisters couldn't act worth a darn.

As Laurel's gaze followed Conner, Jack began to knead the kinks out of her shoulders. "I want to talk to you after the game."

Ominous-sounding words. Apprehensive, she turned to face him. He looked serious. He didn't look like a man who wanted to talk about a future together.

That was it, she thought, despair settling into her stomach. He'd guessed how she felt about him and was going to let her down gently. Tell her they'd had a swell time, but he had to move on.

And they hadn't had a swell time, not with three chaperons living with them.

Laurel stared hard at Jack, searching for some tenderness, some hint of affection. It wasn't there.

She was cold and her mouth tasted sour. Quickly, she tried a sip of the tea, but a lump had formed in her throat.

If ever Laurel had doubted that what she felt for Jack was true till-death-do-us-part love, she doubted no longer.

She couldn't imagine a day without Jack. She'd miss his teasing, his candor and unabashed enthusiasm.

She'd miss learning from him. As he taught her the finer points of poker, they'd discussed psychology, strategy, philosophy and mathematics. He got along with her family, he looked great in a tux and he made her toes tingle. What more could she want in a man?

A commitment. The answer occurred to her immediately. She and Jack had discussed where they'd been in their lives, but never where they were going. When she'd returned to Dallas, she'd had no future plans. She still didn't. But she was ready to make some with Jack.

She managed a smile. "Okay. You want to talk—we'll talk."

He looked as if he wanted to say more. Goodness knows, she *wanted* him to say more, but the other players were moving toward the game table. Laurel bit her lip, then with a shrug and a resigned expression, joined the men.

What had Jack wanted to say to her? Her mind whirring, Laurel sat in the leather club chair. B.J. insisted on changing places with Conner. Mac looked as if he would rather quit than sit next to Conner. Lane fidgeted and Slim handed him the unopened deck of cards. "Your deal."

Lane shuffled and offered the cards to be cut. Play began.

Laurel couldn't concentrate on the game and, not surprisingly, her playing was horrible.

She could only think about her approaching talk with Jack. She was certain he was going to say goodbye. How could she convince him that he needed her?

Unfortunately, as the hour progressed, it was more a case of her needing Jack. Her pile of chips dwindled. Adam and her sisters had abandoned all pretense of indifference and watched, unsmiling.

Conner dealt and Laurel studied him closely, detecting nothing unusual. She glanced at Jack, but he was pouring a glass of iced tea.

Then she saw her hand. Three jacks. She could get a full house if luck ran her way and, if not, she still had the three jacks.

The jack of hearts wasn't one of the cards. Laurel decided it was pure superstition on her part to notice.

Play proceeded around the table, and no one else bet before her. When it was her turn, Laurel tossed some chips into the center of the table. She hadn't even counted them until they left her fingers. Chips no longer represented money to her. They were just chips, with blue worth more than red and red worth more than white.

Maybe she shouldn't have been so extravagant with the blue chips. She didn't have all that many.

She caught a movement out of the corner of her eye and looked up. Jack was frowning.

Had she done something wrong? He'd said to watch Conner, and she had. Had the others noticed something she hadn't?

No. She was being too conservative again. She needed to take more chances.

Laurel swallowed as Conner, wearing a half smile, matched her bet and raised.

She could feel Jack staring at her as she matched Conner's raise to remain in the round.

The room was unnaturally quiet.

"Cards?"

Laurel slid the two cards she wanted to trade out in front of her.

Conner dealt her two cards.

A pair of fours, giving her a full house.

An omen. It had to be. She stared at her cards, as if they would disappear if she looked up.

Conner took one card. "Your bet."

Laurel didn't need to be reminded and was irritated that Conner had done so. She quickly stifled her irritation. She *needed* to concentrate. Conner had more chips than she did. Laurel suspected that he'd force her to call or bet every last chip on this one hand so that if she lost, she'd be out of the game.

Suddenly Laurel wanted it to be finished—the tension, the strain she felt between Jack and herself, the bickering among her sisters, the sly, confident looks of Conner, the whispers of the other men—she'd had enough.

"There you are, Conner." Using both hands, she pushed all her chips into the pot. "Shall I gift wrap them?"

Laurel hadn't withdrawn her hands before Conner began counting out a matching pile of chips from his own stack.

She didn't want to prolong the suspense and flipped her cards. "Jacks over fours."

Dispassionately, Conner spread out his own full house. Three kings and two nines. He'd won. Strangely, Laurel felt relief.

It was finished.

"Break," B.J. said into the silence.

Laurel offered her hand to Conner, tugging it away when she realized he was going to kiss it instead of shake it.

"I think I'd like some air," she announced to no one in particular.

She made her way blindly down the hall to the door off the back staircase.

The cool air felt good against her heated cheeks. Almost immediately, the door opened and someone came to stand beside her on the tiny back porch.

Jack.

Laurel spoke first. "I lost."

"I know."

The numbness, the relief, began to wear off. "It's over." To her surprise, her voice cracked. She'd thought she was handling everything so well, so calmly.

"Do you know why you lost?"

"Because he had a better hand." Laurel sighed and heard a quiver. "But I had three jacks!"

"I'm not surprised. Conner probably dealt you a good hand to lure you in."

It took a moment for Laurel to understand. "You think he cheated?" Losing was bad enough, but to lose because Conner had cheated was intolerable. "How?"

Jack shrugged. "Conner's a card mechanic. Didn't you notice the others weren't betting?"

Laurel nodded. "But..." She had been about to argue, but what was the point? She'd promised Jack she'd only play Conner once. Even though Conner had cheated, she'd promised. "I guess my inexperience showed."

"Yeah." Jack reached a hand under her hair and rubbed the nape of her neck.

He meant it was a gesture of comfort, Laurel knew, but the sizzle that flashed down her spine and settled between her toes instantly reminded her of the reason she'd wanted to finish playing in the first place—she and Jack needed to discuss life after The Game.

Laurel curled herself into his side and rested her head against him. She'd think about losing later.

Jack didn't say anything; he merely ran his hand up and down her arm.

What was he waiting for? A cue? Okay, she was good with cues. "You wanted to talk?"

She could hear him swallow. She swallowed, too.

He took a deep breath. "Do you remember your promise not to play Conner anymore?"

"Was that what you wanted to discuss with me?" Laurel pushed herself away from him.

"Among other things."

"I gave you my word. I know it means I have to face Holly and Ivy as a loser, but I gave you my word. You're always emphasizing the worth of your word—why are you doubting mine?" Why were they quarreling? She didn't want to quarrel.

"Laurel, I don't doubt that you meant your promise. I just wonder if you can live with it."

"You mean because he cheated? I'm handling myself okay, aren't I?" She wrapped her arms around herself and hopped down the two concrete steps.

"A little too okay. I expected . . ."

"What?" Laurel turned to look up at him. "Wailing and gnashing of teeth?"

Jack nodded. "Kind of."

"I'm a big girl. I can take losing," she muttered.

Jack looked doubtful.

"What's the matter?"

"Under the circumstances, I'm surprised you can ask," he said, slowly descending the steps.

"Do you *want* me to break my promise? Are you looking for an excuse to stick around?"

Jack shoved his hands into the back pockets of his pants and stared up at the stars. "I wasn't aware that I needed one."

"You don't. But you've made it quite clear that you can't wait to leave." Laurel hadn't meant to add that last part.

"That's not true."

"Isn't that why you made me promise not to play Conner more than once?"

For a moment, Laurel thought he wouldn't answer her. He scuffed the gravel next to the driveway with the toe of his loafer. "I don't want to see you and your family become obsessed with Conner. I don't want to see you lose thousands of dollars trying to beat him. Winning against him can't ever make up for what you think he did to your family."

"What we *think?* Don't you believe us?" Laurel began to pace. "Ivy researched Conner. Holly has heard gossip. Adam had access to court records. This wasn't a project we started just to amuse ourselves during the holidays." Laurel tried to overcome her anger. Why couldn't they stop fighting? She didn't want to be angry with Jack.

"I know that. I simply think it's time your family quit dwelling on the past." Jack's voice became louder to match hers. "I don't want you to chase Conner all over the country challenging him to poker matches."

As if she would. "What does it matter to you, anyway?" She was practically shouting.

"Damn it, I love you!" he shouted back, looking as frustrated as she felt. "And that *wasn't* the way I'd intended to tell you!"

The echoes faded into silence as they stared at each other.

He loved her! Joy of joys, he loved her! Conner no longer mattered. She grinned so widely her cheeks hurt. "I was afraid you were toying with my affections," she said in an exaggerated Southern drawl. "I thought you wanted to leave."

Jack reached out to caress her cheek. "I want to leave, all right, but I want to take you with me."

Laurel shivered with happiness. "You know I'm crazy about you, of course."

"No." Jack laughed and held out his arms.

Laurel hurled herself against his chest, then, standing on tiptoe, stretched herself until she and Jack were eye to eye, nose to nose... and mouth to mouth.

"I'm absolutely obsessed with you," she whispered against his lips.

Jack caught her breath and whispered back to her, "I like the sound of that."

He tried to kiss her, but Laurel was so happy she just had to smile. Chuckling deep in her throat, she threw back her head and surrendered to the laughter. "Oh, Jack! If only I'd known how you felt *before* I had to play cards, I would have been able to concentrate. Who knows? I might have won."

She felt him stiffen and her laughter died.

"You'll never forget, will you?"

Laurel knew he meant the game. "No, but it makes no difference."

"I don't think I believe you." He pulled her close again. "If you'd won, that would have been the end of it, but Conner is still between us, isn't he?"

"Too soon to tell." But as she said the words, Laurel realized she was lying. Conner, the cheat, *was* still there. Unfinished business.

"I saw your sisters' faces. They're going to try to persuade you to play Conner again."

Laurel thought of Holly and Ivy and knew Jack was right. "I'll say no."

"Will you?" He searched her face in the moonlight.

"I promised you, didn't I?" she asked lightly, trying not to think about Conner.

"Will you regret promising?"

"No," she answered while she still could. She should be deliriously happy. Jack loved her. She loved Jack.

The knowledge didn't make her heart sing, not any-more.

All the love she felt for him was being smothered by her bitterness toward Conner. Hadn't she suffered enough be-cause of Conner? But maybe he'd lose to one of the oth-ers. That would make her feel better, wouldn't it? "How much longer will this game go on?"

Jack shrugged. "A couple more hours."

Laurel eased herself away from him and took his hand. "Let's go watch."

He hesitated, studying her. "Are you ready to face your sisters?"

Holly. Laurel visualized Holly's face and Adam's, too. The money she'd lost belonged to them. She imagined Ivy's disappointment. Ivy had looked up to her.

Reaction began to set in with a vengeance. She'd *lost*. She'd lost because she'd been cheated—the way her father had been cheated in his business. The way her parents had been cheated of their lives. And now, after all the practic-ing, the big showdown was over and Conner had won again. By cheating.

For a moment, Laurel was able to hold Jack's gaze, then she squeezed her eyes shut. "I can't stand it. Losing is one thing, but being cheated is . . . just not fair!" She sounded like a little kid. "Maybe if you taught me how to play with cheaters—"

Jack grabbed her shoulders and shook her slightly. Laurel could feel the tension in his hands and knew he wanted to shake her until her teeth rattled, or until she be-gan thinking another way. His way.

"I knew it." He released her, balling his hands into fists at his side. "This thing with Conner will be between us forever, won't it?" He ran his fingers through his hair. "We'll have this argument again and again."

"That's because it's not resolved." And it never could be resolved because of Laurel's promise.

"But everything would be terrific if you'd won?"

"Or if Conner loses tonight."

Jack made a derisive sound. "Not a chance. None of those guys has ever beaten Conner."

"You have."

Until she saw Jack's face, frozen into a disbelieving expression, Laurel was unaware that she'd spoken aloud.

They stood motionless, gazing at each other for a long time in the moonlight. The air was crisp and cool, and the stars twinkled.

Laurel's heart beat a quick cadence as she waited for Jack to speak. Deep, deep inside, she'd known she wasn't good enough to compete with that group. It would take months, maybe years, of actual game experience, which she didn't have.

But Jack did.

"So *that's* it. You want me to play Conner."

For a brief moment, Laurel allowed herself to hope.

"You know what you're asking of me?" His voice was a hoarse whisper.

"I'm not—"

"You couldn't love me or you wouldn't ask me to play him."

"I'm not asking you to play. Forget it." One part of Laurel was horrified that she had even thought of Jack challenging Conner to a game. The other part whispered that if he really loved her, he'd play Conner for her, for their future.

"If I don't play Conner you'll never forgive me," Jack said in a remote voice, almost as if he was thinking aloud.

"I'll forgive—"

"Forgive?"

"Jack! That was your word!"

"And obviously appropriate."

Laurel exhaled in exasperation. "I won't lie and say that the thought of you playing never occurred to me, but I understand how you feel about gambling."

"There are no guarantees," Jack said, as he had before. "I could lose."

Was he worried about being out of practice? Did he doubt his abilities? "You wouldn't lose," Laurel reassured him automatically, the way he'd reassured her countless times before. "You're better than anyone here tonight." She moved to encircle him with her arms, but he shrugged her off. Hurt, she glanced up at him. His expression was stony and his eyes were the color of pale jade. He looked exactly the way he had the night he'd defeated her to teach her a lesson.

"How can you profess to love someone, and ask him to do something that will hurt him? If I were an alcoholic, would you insist I drink champagne at our wedding reception?"

She'd made a terrible mistake. Jack hadn't been seeking reassurance. What could she have been thinking of? "You're right," she murmured. "You're right, you're right. I'm so sorry." This time, she succeeded in wrapping her arms around him and planting tiny kisses over his jaw.

Groaning, Jack captured her mouth beneath his, and they clung together, silently apologizing, comforting and healing.

"Consoling the loser, Hartman?"

Jack and Laurel wrenched apart so quickly Laurel felt actual pain.

Conner, hands in his pockets, regarded them unblinkingly. "Play's starting up again." His eyes flicked toward Laurel, then returned to Jack. "There's an empty seat."

"No, thank you," Laurel said, her voice firm and loud. She glared at Conner, allowing every ounce of the hate she felt to show in her face. Maybe if she glared her hate, she'd exorcize the bitterness.

Once again, Conner's gaze briefly met hers, then swiveled to Jack.

Laurel squeezed Jack's arm to tell him to forget Conner. The sooner they all forgot Conner, the sooner they could get on with their lives.

The two men stared at each other for long moments, then Conner turned and strolled toward the house. Reaching the doorway, he stopped, his back to them. "Coming, Hartman?"

Jack looked down at Laurel. "Save me a chair," he replied, hesitating no longer than a heartbeat. "I'm in."

CHAPTER ELEVEN

LAUREL WAITED until Conner nodded his silver head and closed the door. "Jack, don't!"

Jack gazed at her beautiful face. Did she have any idea how expressive it was? He'd seen the pure hatred radiating from her eyes as she'd looked at Conner. He'd seen the flash of hope when he'd agreed to play.

"Jack, please." She clutched his arm. "Conner was trying to goad you into playing him. He's always wanted to play you—not me."

Her protest sounded sincere, but of course she was an actress. "So now he gets his wish. And so do you."

"But he cheats!"

"That didn't concern you when you asked me to play him a few minutes ago."

Laurel's hand slid from his arm, and she visibly censored her first impulsive retort. "I never asked—"

"Yes, you did." Jack was tired of the discussion, the wrangling. "Those big brown eyes looked at me and said, 'Please, Jack, please play him for me.'"

Laurel bowed her head, hiding those same brown eyes. "I've already apologized."

"I know. And we've talked about the game, your playing and my playing until I'm sick of it."

"Let's drop it then!" Laurel snapped.

"Okay." Jack crossed his arms over his chest and waited. She wouldn't be able to forget the game. She wouldn't be able to let go.

Laurel tossed her hair over her shoulder, fidgeting. Someone walking down the hallway blocked the light spilling from the windows.

Jack saw Laurel's quick glance at the house. She bit her lip, then released it and composed her face when she remembered he was watching.

"You can't forget the game, can you?"

She took a deep breath. "Is that so surprising?"

Jack looked through the windows at the people milling around. "Every time you're quiet, I'll wonder if you're thinking about this game." His eyes returned to hers. "Every time you think of your family, you'll remember this game. Every time you see me, you'll think of this game."

"Give me some credit for having a few other interests!"

Other interests? Since he'd met her, Laurel and her family had worked single-mindedly toward confronting Conner.

Jack was their tool.

Admitting it to himself unearthed a few painful questions. He decided to ask one. "Will you love me more if I win?"

She looked outraged. "I hope you meant that as a joke!"

"Actually, no."

"My feelings for you have nothing to do with playing poker."

Jack doubted that. He stood closer, noting Laurel's involuntary step backward. "What if I lose? Will you still love me?"

Laurel drew a shaky breath. "Actually, right now—"

"You're not certain you love me at all."

"That wasn't what I was going to say!"

"It doesn't matter." He had his answer. She hadn't said she loved him. She'd mentioned her feelings, being crazy about him, but no "I love you, Jack."

Where was the zing? The fireworks?

Frankly, as a love scene, this stank.

Jack reached out, tilted Laurel's chin and kissed her on the forehead. "It's not whether I win or lose, it's *if* I play the game."

He walked back into the house, leaving her there, standing in the moonlight. He had a poker game to play.

He'd been stupid to tell Laurel he loved her. And he did love her. Who wouldn't? He remembered the defeated woman with the dingy hair playing on his sympathies. He remembered her transformation into a beautiful, but appealingly insecure, butterfly. He'd rebuilt her confidence and convinced her—and himself—that she was a desirable woman.

What an actress. Too bad she couldn't play a love scene.

Jack headed toward the den, his loafers sounding a countdown on the parquet floor.

He stepped into the room, immediately struck by the heat and stale smells of smoke, food and ten bodies that had been closeted together for several hours.

It was a familiar atmosphere, one he'd never thought he'd experience again. Jack stood behind the chair Laurel had vacated and inhaled deeply, as the memories rushed back. Then he sat down, surrendering to them.

The men had played several hands by the time Laurel reentered the room. Jack was vaguely aware of the whispered conference between Laurel and her sisters, but he couldn't spare them any mental energy now. He was becoming reacquainted with all the old feelings he'd fought for so long: the anticipation of a good hand, the disappointment of losing, the satisfaction of winning. The actual fun he was having.

Maybe that's what had been wrong. Poker had stopped being fun and started becoming work. There wasn't any reason he couldn't play in moderation, was there?

Jack felt his blood chill when he realized the direction of his thoughts.

He'd only been playing for half an hour! Years of coping had nearly been erased.

How could she have asked him to play?

Why had he agreed?

Jack shot a look toward Laurel. The reasons for playing weren't important. All that mattered was that he *was* playing.

Laurel had a pinched expression on her face. Guilt? Regret?

Or, he thought cynically, disappointment because he wasn't winning big yet?

Had she been using him all along? Was this what her family had planned—not for Laurel to play, but for Jack to beat Conner?

IT WAS CONNER'S DEAL and Laurel endured Jack's stare.

Okay, he'd made his point. She noticed that neither he nor the others were betting. Conner didn't seem bothered and nonchalantly raked in the antes.

During each deal, Laurel had to suffer Jack's black look. He was absolutely livid with her and she felt appropriately awful. How many times did she have to apologize?

She's made a mistake. Yes, a big one, but she hadn't pretended to be perfect. She wasn't wearing a halo. If Jack expected perfection, then no wonder he was disappointed.

"He hates me," she said in an undertone to Holly.

"Who? Conner?"

"Jack."

Holly studied Jack before replying. "I'm surprised he's playing after he warned us about Conner."

Laurel moaned as guilt engulfed her. "It's my fault. We were talking about the game and I said I just wanted *somebody* to beat Conner and, well, Jack is the only one here who can."

Holly jerked her head to stare at Laurel. "*You* asked him to play?"

"Conner did the asking, but . . ."

But Laurel had been fooling herself. Jack was playing for her. She'd whined and griped. She was supposed to be an actress. She should have been able to convince him that she had no further interest in beating Conner.

She met Jack's stormy eyes with another apology in hers.

He glared. She couldn't stand it. At the next opportunity, she moved behind him where she could see his cards and not the hard look in his eyes.

As she watched Jack play, Laurel realized that there was no substitute for experience. Poker was a game of skill. Luck played a small part.

The tempo of the game increased. The men talked in short, sharp bursts. Those who wanted to smoke, smoked. Earlier, in deference to Holly's condition, they had taken more frequent breaks and stepped outside.

More than an hour had passed since Laurel had seen Jack's face. He now had a large pile of chips in front of him, about the same size as Conner's.

"I'm out," B.J. announced. "How about a drink?"

The others agreed on a quick break, too, and silently ambled toward the leather-topped bar, where Adam acted as bartender.

"Jack might win. He might actually win!" Ivy whispered.

"That's not important," Laurel snapped.

"What are you saying?" Ivy asked just as Jack sauntered by. Laurel could tell that he had overheard, and his scornful expression cut right through her.

Ignoring Ivy, Laurel followed him to the bar. "Jack, please quit. You've played enough."

His eyes narrowed. "I haven't won all his money, Laurel. How can it be enough?"

His tone was harsh and strained, his face weary.

She had done this to him. Tears stung her throat. "I don't want you to play anymore."

"Don't you?" Jack swallowed the last of a soda.

"No!" Her urgent whisper attracted a few glances. "I don't care if you win or lose."

"Really?" He spoke without emotion, and Laurel gave up trying to blink back the tears. They overflowed, spilling down her cheeks.

She watched Jack's eyes follow the path of one teardrop. When it reached her jaw, he flicked it away with his index finger. "What a performance."

As Laurel gasped, he spun on his heel and rejoined the game.

Performance? He thought she was acting? The only acting she was doing was convincing Holly and Ivy that she still cared about the game's outcome one way or another. And she didn't care anymore, she realized. She honestly didn't care.

Laurel took a deep breath, relief making her light-headed. She *could* let go.

Life wasn't always fair. There were no guarantees.

As her thoughts echoed Jack's frequent caveat, goose-flesh rose on her arms.

Jack.

Across the room, he settled down to play, a hard-faced man with a world-weary air. That wasn't her Jack. Her Jack possessed a contagious enthusiasm, a sharp mind and a teasing sense of humor.

But that Jack was gone and she might never see him again.

Laurel closed her eyes. A poker game wasn't all she'd lost tonight. Her breath caught on a sob. Jack wouldn't even look at her now. The only feeling he had left for her was contempt.

In spite of herself, Laurel was drawn back to the poker game, where she took up a somber vigil. One by one, the other players withdrew, but stayed to watch the contest unfold between Jack and Conner.

Slim, the last to leave the table except for Conner and Jack, came to stand beside Laurel and her sisters. "He's a slippery one, but Jack'll get him."

Laurel smiled, weakly at first, then stronger as Jack glanced at her.

Fine. If Jack was going to play, then Laurel would show him that she supported him. She was going to smile and smile big.

She positioned herself so that she could see Jack's cards and the side of his face, then composed a pleased and interested expression for herself.

The game went back and forth, but each time Jack looked her way, she wore the same wide smile. *See,* she tried to tell him, *it really doesn't matter.*

"You look like you're auditioning for a toothpaste commercial," Ivy whispered.

"I'm trying to show Jack our support. How do you think he feels if we all stand around with gloomy expressions?"

Ivy blinked as she digested Laurel's words. "You're right." She grinned at Jack and waved.

A slightly green Holly managed a sickly smile. Adam rolled his eyes, gave Jack a thumbs-up and retreated to the kitchen.

LOOK AT THEM all beaming at him. They thought he was ready to wipe Conner out.

Jack was deeply disappointed with them, especially Laurel. It had been a long time since he'd been taken in by a pair of long legs, pretty brown eyes and a hard-luck story.

He wanted out. He'd had enough. It didn't even matter that Conner had quit cheating.

His next hand held nothing of value. He glanced sideways at Laurel. Her silly smile irritated him. He knew she could see his cards, so he bet heavily, just to needle her.

Conner matched his bet, then raised. So did Jack. It was idiocy. The pot was worth thousands of dollars.

Conner stood pat, Jack exchanged two cards and Laurel still smiled. As did Ivy and Holly. What was wrong with them? Didn't they see the absurd bets he'd made?

Oh, now he understood. They wanted him to believe that they didn't care if he won or lost so he wouldn't crack under the pressure.

He'd show them pressure.

Jack looked straight at Laurel, to make sure she was watching, and shoved his remaining chips into the center of the table.

Her eyes glazed, but her smile only got wider.

Then she blew him a kiss.

Startled, he turned his head away just in time to realize that Conner had witnessed the whole thing.

Of course, Conner didn't know that Jack had bet all his chips without cards to back them up. It was a pure bluff— if Conner called, Jack had no chance of winning.

Conner sat motionless for endless moments.

Jack knew Conner could match the bet and still have some chips left over, a fact Jack wished he'd considered earlier.

He almost regretted his impulsive bet. It was against everything he'd taught Laurel about betting and bluffing. It was stupid.

He watched Conner consider him. Then he watched Conner look at Laurel and her family.

And then he watched Conner fold.

Fold?

From a long way off, Jack heard clapping and laughing.

Conner had thrown in his cards without calling Jack's bluff?

Jack stared in disbelief at the mountain of chips in the center of the table. He'd tried to lose and he'd won. Conner must have thought those big smiles meant Jack had a good hand.

He looked at Laurel and her family, now wearing real smiles, and felt an urgent desire to win every last chip from Conner.

Victory didn't take long. Conner had been shaken by his enormous loss and confused by the change in Jack's style of playing.

With each hand, Jack became more daring, more like the old Jack he'd described to Laurel. The actual end of the game was anticlimactic, but no less satisfying than the thrill he'd felt at his unintentionally successful bluff.

He still had the knack. Jack Hartman could hold his own with the best of them. He smiled to himself.

"I play in a Tuesday-night game down in Houston," Conner said, standing slowly. "Can you make it?"

Jack glanced up eagerly, about to accept, when a feminine voice spoke. "Sorry, Conner. Jack will be busy." Laurel slipped her arms around him and nuzzled his neck.

Laurel's touch jolted him back to reality. Reality was that he no longer played poker. He shouldn't play poker. In spite of his win today, he had to remember how it felt when he lost.

And he had to remember Laurel. What if she wanted to play Conner again? What if she wanted *him* to play Conner again? No matter what they said, the Hall sisters wouldn't be satisfied unless Conner was destroyed. Maybe they didn't know it, but Jack did.

He patted Laurel's arm. "I'll be busy Tuesday, but how about another hand right now? Double or nothing?"

There was immediate quiet. Laurel's arms tightened convulsively. Jack pried them off and shoved the deck of cards across the table, his gaze locked with Conner's. "Your deal."

"Jack!" Laurel sounded frantic.

"Jack." Adam's voice contained a warning.

Holly and Ivy's mouths were open, but silent.

Conner, eyes hooded, resumed his seat at the table and shuffled the cards.

Jack caught the gazes of the other players and signaled them to watch. They edged closer.

Conner offered the deck to be cut and Jack tapped it once. Raising a brow in surprise, Conner began to deal.

Jack stared at Conner's hands as the cards slid from them. The distraction provided during the shuffle, coupled with Jack's refusing the cut, would tempt an honest man. Conner wasn't an honest man.

One...two...

And there it was. The slightest of movements indicating that Conner was dealing seconds—dealing the second card from the pack and keeping the top one for himself.

Jack slammed Conner's wrist to the table. Conner grunted in pain.

A woman screamed.

Jack smiled. "Not this time." He moved back slightly so everyone could see Conner's right thumb stopped in the act of drawing out the second card.

Conner's fingers were turning purple; his face was turning white.

"You a number-two man, Conner?" Slim flipped over the card Conner was keeping for himself. A king.

Conner didn't bother with denials. "Enough, Hartman." He sat back in the chair, rubbing his wrist after Jack released it, and regarded each of the players. "Name your price," he said, obviously believing they had one.

Everyone looked at Jack. Jack looked at Laurel.

Her chin raised. "My father's life. My mother's life. My father's reputation. The family business," she enunciated clearly.

Jack was proud of her. She had grasped the situation immediately without the hysterical ravings to which she was entitled.

Conner snorted. "That's all in the past. Dead and gone."

Jack stood gazing down at the silver-haired man. "And so are your poker-playing days."

The first signs of panic appeared in Conner's eyes. "I'm a wealthy man."

"And a cheat," Laurel said. "Cheaters aren't welcome here." She strode to the double front door and flung it wide. The cool night air rushed into the overheated room.

Jack smiled at the dramatic gesture. Vintage Laurel.

Still Conner sat at the table, attempting to maintain dignity even when faced with social ruin. "Please."

Jack arched an eyebrow at the others, though he knew what their response would be. They were all wealthy men. They played poker because they loved the game. After today, Conner would never again play with the poker elite.

Slim answered for them. "It's not your first time cheating, Conner. It's just your first time getting caught."

The faint hope died in Conner's eyes. He knew—they all knew—that by tomorrow, not a decent game in the entire country would be open to him. He rose stiffly from the table, stumbling once on his way toward the door. Reaching it, he faced Laurel. "I told him not to fly out to that well."

Laurel turned her head away, tears spilling down her cheeks.

Conner, without looking back, walked into the night.

Laurel's shoulders heaved, and Ivy and Holly ran to the door, slamming it shut. The three sisters clung together.

Jack drew a long breath, easing the cramped muscles in his shoulders. "Fair maidens, I've slain your dragon." They didn't hear him. "Now I've got to slay mine."

They didn't hear that, either.

"JACK, ARE YOU IN HERE? Come celebrate with us," Laurel called from the doorway of his room just as he emerged from the closet with an armload of clothes.

Suitcases were open on the bed and the floor. "Are you leaving?" He couldn't leave. Not now.

"Isn't it time?"

"We have to talk—about us."

Jack stuffed his clothes into the luggage. "Cut the act, Laurel. You got what you wanted—even more."

"No, I didn't." She had to stop him. "I want you."

He threw her a look of disgust. "You don't know what you want." He zipped the suitcases and unplugged his computer.

As he watched him, Laurel felt helpless. She had to do something. "Where are you going?"

"Away. Away from temptation, if you will." He smiled in self-derision.

She hated seeing him like this. Hated knowing she was responsible. "Let me come with you."

"So you can tend to my wounds?" He snapped the computer case shut. "No, thanks."

What more could she say? The closer Jack came to leaving, the more Laurel knew she wanted him to stay. "I realized, while you were playing, that I no longer cared about what Conner did."

"Better late than never." Jack scanned the room, grabbed a stray sock and zipped up the last of his suitcases.

In less than half an hour, he had eliminated every trace of his occupancy.

"Stop!" Laurel swallowed and abandoned her pride, something she'd held on to during all her struggles in California. Pride had seemed important then. But not anymore. "You said you loved me."

"Don't rub it in."

"And I told you I loved you!"

Jack grabbed a couple of suitcases. "No, you didn't."

Was that the problem? "But I do. I do love you!"

Jack closed his eyes and took a deep breath. "Are you going to give me a hand with these or not?"

Laurel marched over to the largest of the remaining suitcases and sat on it. "No."

Jack shrugged and headed downstairs.

She was not going to let him walk out of her life without a fight. She dug in her heels and waited.

Jack returned, eyed her silently, hoisted a carry-on bag over his shoulder, picked up the computer and left the room.

Nothing of his remained, except the suitcase Laurel had commandeered.

"Are you going to get off that now?" he asked when he climbed the stairs for the third time.

"No. Not until we talk about us."

Jack sighed heavily. "There never was an us. That was an illusion you created. I don't want an illusion. I want a real woman."

"I am real!" The game had twisted his thinking.

He stared down at her. "What are your plans now that the evil Conner has been vanquished?"

"I—I don't have any."

"What do you want to do with the rest of your life?"

Be with you, Laurel thought, achingly aware that she had failed to convince him her feelings were genuine.

Jack shook his head, taking her silence as indecision. "Now, last warning—off the luggage, or I'll jerk it out from under you."

"I'm not moving until you give me a chance to explain."

"Okay." Jack squatted next to her.

Laurel opened her mouth, thinking he was ready to listen.

Instead of listening, Jack tugged sharply on the end of the suitcase and sent her tumbling to the floor.

"Hey!" She glared at him furiously.

He started down the stairs, suitcase in hand.

Laurel picked herself up and followed him, shouting, "You're running away, Jack! It won't do any good." She pushed past her family, in a cluster at the bottom of the stairs, and chased Jack out the kitchen door.

"I'm going to track you down and make you hear me out!"

Jack spared her a brief glance as he crammed the suitcase into his car. "You gotta find me first."

"You love me!"

"I'll get over it." He slid into the Jaguar and slammed the door shut.

Laurel ran to the car and knocked on the window until he lowered it. "I won't let you."

Jack twisted the ignition switch. "I'll give you some advice—decide what you want to do with your life." He adjusted the mirror. "Then do it."

He was just going to drive off. Laurel leaned inside and kissed him. If he left, he'd leave with something to think about.

Jack resisted at first, then his hand cupped the back of her head and his lips ground against hers.

A kiss of desperation on her part quickly changed into something more. Energy flowed between them. Laurel felt vibrantly alive.

Jack moaned deep in his throat, sending flutters of hope through her.

Laurel kissed Jack as if her life depended on it, because right then, she wasn't sure it didn't.

Jack wrenched himself away from her. "I don't ever want to see you again," he said quietly, then turned to stare straight ahead, both hands gripping the steering wheel.

Laurel didn't move. "You love me, Jack. You can't leave me this way."

Jack shifted the car into gear. "I wouldn't bet on it."

"How much of a hike?" Laurel stared at the grizzled man in the plaid shirt who weighed scoops of foul-smelling bait.

"Mile . . . mile and a quarter depending on your turns."

"But I've got stuff to carry." Laurel stepped outside the bait shop and looked at the dense forest. "Where's the path?"

The man laughed. "Anywhere you want."

"How will I find his cabin?" she asked, as she returned to the counter.

"Walk northwest until you bump into it." Without wiping his hands, the man pulled out a compass from a glass case and gave it to her.

Laurel accepted the black disk gingerly. "Thanks."

"Four ninety-five."

"Oh." She nodded and opened her purse.

"Gonna wear those?" The man gestured at her ostrich-skin boots.

"I don't have any other appropriate footwear," Laurel informed him, an edge to her voice.

The man grunted and disappeared into the curtained back room, returning with a pair of hiking boots and two pairs of thick socks. "Try these."

The boots were too wide, but adequate if she wore both pairs of socks at the same time.

While Laurel tried on the boots, the plaid-shirted man added a backpack and a bright orange vest to the pile.

When he tossed a wicked-looking knife onto the counter, she protested, "What's that for?"

"You got a gun?"

"No!"

"Animals."

Fear jolted through her. "There're animals out there?"

The man started laughing, loud guffaws that revealed yellow teeth. He wheezed and banged the counter with his hand, bouncing the worms in their moist soil. "Animals!" he whooped. Then he slid down out of sight.

Great. She should have been a comedian. "I'll just carry a big stick."

The worst thing, Laurel thought as she paid the chuckling man, was that she might have to hike back—alone.

Once she was in the trees, she realized they weren't as close together as she'd thought, and she even fancied that she saw a faint trail. It meandered in a northwesterly direction, so she followed it.

"Jack had better appreciate this," she chanted, marching along, though the chant became more of a snarl the heavier her backpack felt.

In spite of walking, she was cold. Texas clothes weren't made to withstand winters in upstate New York. Besides, in Dallas, late February had some balmy days.

The hiking boots made her feet weigh a ton each. Who needed aerobics classes when they wore these?

Laurel stopped to catch her breath and became aware of a faint smoky smell scenting the crisp air.

Well, somebody was around here. Checking her compass, Laurel kept trudging along, thinking of the amused Paul Bunyan look-alike at the bait shop and his scanty directions. Had she gone far enough?

Then she spotted the cabin.

Laurel stopped. Had she found Jack's cabin or some sex-starved hunter's?

Great time to think of that, Laurel. Slipping her backpack from her shoulders, Laurel—and her stick—quietly approached the cabin. She couldn't see any windows on this side. Creeping quietly, moist leaves cushioning the sound of her hiking boots, Laurel circled the cabin until she found a grimy window.

She held her breath and listened.

Silence.

Using one gloved hand, she wiped a small spot and stood on her toes to peer inside.

And came face-to-face with a bearded man.

Laurel gasped, dropped her stick and began to run.

Or attempted to run. The heavy hiking boots slowed her considerably, and when she tried to leap over a log, she couldn't raise her foot high enough and she tripped, tumbling into the musty foliage carpeting the ground.

Hands closed around her shoulders and lifted.

She kicked out.

"Hey!"

Laurel whipped her head back to stare into a bearded face with money-colored eyes.

"Jack?" Relief, blessed relief, slowed her racing heart. She scrambled into a sitting position. "I didn't recognize you with your beard."

"What are you doing here?" He grinned at her. A good sign.

"Being a real woman." She stood, brushing off the damp leaves. "A woman who decides what she wants and goes after it. Aggressive, independent." She flexed her muscles. "Strong."

"I wasn't looking for Superwoman."

"Good. I can't leap tall logs in a single bound."

His teeth flashed in a quick smile. It was hidden somewhat beneath the beard, but it was there nonetheless. "Come inside."

Nervously, Laurel grabbed her backpack, hauled it to her shoulders and followed Jack into the cabin. There was one room and a bathroom, standard rustic furniture, Jack's computer—looking out of place—and a bunk bed.

Ignoring the chair in front of the computer, Laurel sat on a heavy chest near the fireplace. The glowing coals and lazy flames warmed her back.

Jack, hands on hips, watched her.

"What's with the beards and the plaid?" She pointed to his flannel shirt. "Is this some kind of male thing?"

"How did you find me?" he asked, ignoring her question.

"Ivy and I thought long and hard. We read books on the psychology of the wounded male and plotted every possible location—"

"You called my mother."

"Lovely woman." Laurel glanced at him coyly. "She wants grandchildren."

Jack groaned. "What did you tell her?"

Laurel smiled. "That I'd do my best." She batted her eyelashes.

Jack looked at her sternly and sat on the one chair. "Okay, Laurel. Why are you here and what is all that stuff?" He poked her backpack with his foot.

She swallowed. "If you refused to answer the door, I planned to lure you outside with the smell of *huevos rancheros.*"

He stuck out his lower lip and nodded. "Might have worked. Then what?"

"Then I'd tell you what I planned to do with my life." Organizing her life had taken her every day of the six weeks, four days and who knew how many hours since he'd left, but she'd done it and, by golly, he'd better listen to her now.

He tilted his head to one side. "So tell me, Laurel, what do you plan to do with your life?"

There was a faintly sarcastic air about him, but Laurel plowed ahead. "Ivy and I made a list of all my qualifications. I have a business degree, I've studied acting, I'm good at sales, and I decorate a mean Christmas tree." She paused, expecting a chuckle at that last part.

Not even a smile.

"So—" she reached into her pocket and withdrew a slightly wilted card "—voilà."

Jack read the card. "The Laurel Hall Agency? Actors' Representative?"

"Yes. I could always pick the best person for the part, and while I enjoy acting, I'm not very good."

"You don't have any experience."

"Yes, I do! I represented Ivy for a hair commercial."

Laurel saw a reluctant smile. "Did she get the part?"

"No, but she got two callbacks."

Jack chuckled, shaking his head. "Congratulations. I wish you all the best."

This did not sound like a declaration of everlasting love. Had she made a mistake in coming here? Had all the sizzle been on her part?

"For my next job, I'm casting a wedding. I've got the bride, matron of honor, bridesmaid and mother of the groom." She bit her lip. "You know, *you* would be just perfect for the part of the groom." Her voice held steady until right at the last.

"Laurel, I can't marry you."

She heard pity in his voice and shut her eyes. How humiliating. How fast could she hike back to the bait shop and her rental car?

She felt Jack touch her arm. "I can't marry anyone. Not after playing in that game. What if I start gambling again?"

Laurel opened her eyes to see the pained expression in his. "I'll keep you too busy," she said, her voice huskier than usual.

Something flared in his eyes, then died. "You deserve better."

"Better than perfect?"

"Oh, Laurel..." His fingers briefly caressed her cheek, then his hand dropped to his side. "I couldn't."

"Even though you love me?"

"*Because* I love you."

He was being noble. She wasn't interested in nobility. "I don't want you to fight all alone. Besides, we'll make a great team. You're a natural for managing other people's money. I know you want to be an independent broker, and we could share an office. I'll help actors earn money. You'll help them spend it."

He was tempted by her idea, she could tell. "It sounds..."

"Like just what you want to do."

His green eyes blazed at her. "More than you could possibly imagine."

Laurel's heart began to pound. "If cards are going to control your life, let them decide this."

"What do you mean?"

Laurel reached into her bag, got out a pack of cards and began to shuffle. "One more game."

"No. Haven't you been listening to me?" Jack knocked his chair over as he hastily put distance between them.

Laurel calmly continued to shuffle. "Cut," she said, slapping the deck on the table.

"No!"

Laurel shrugged and smoothed the cards out in a long line across the polished wood. "One game. One card. High card we get married and live happily ever after. Low card, I hike back right now."

She rested her elbows on the table and waited.

"This is crazy. You're willing to let cards decide your future?"

"Isn't that what you're doing? At least this way, we've got a chance to win."

Jack paced back and forth, muttering to himself. "How can you base a marriage on gambling?" he burst out.

"Jack, honey, marriage is the biggest gamble of them all."

He hesitated, clenching and unclenching his hands, then stormed over to the table. "We get married if I choose a high card and you leave if I draw low?"

She nodded.

"You're bluffing." He looked at her with his poker face.

"So call."

Jack hesitated a long moment. "Okay."

"Remember." She gave him a slow smile. "Jacks are wild."

She saw his chest rise and fall as his breathing increased.

His hand hovered over the line of cards, moving from one end to the other. "Whatever happens?" he asked.

"Whatever happens," she repeated.

Jack tapped a card with his index finger, nudging it out of line. He looked at Laurel once more before flipping it over.

The jack of hearts.

"I don't believe it," he whispered. "Do you see that?"

Laurel nodded, tears already collecting in her eyes.

Jack smiled and held out his arms. "If ever there was a sign—"

He never got a chance to finish because Laurel hurled herself at him.

They melted together with the urgency of two people in love who've been apart for too long. Laurel explored the softness of Jack's beard and inhaled the unfamiliar woodsy smoke smells that clung to him.

The new and the old blended together and she loved it. Loved him. "Jack, I love you. I want to make that clear right now, so you won't accuse me of not saying the words."

Jack smiled ruefully. "I never stopped loving you...even when I was angry. You knew that, didn't you?"

Laurel smiled. "Yeah, but it's nice to hear you say so."

"One thing." Jack sobered. "That was my last game."

Laurel took a deep breath. "Okay." She gestured toward the fireplace. "Then why don't we burn the cards, like I burned my audition dress?"

He grinned his agreement and Laurel hastily gathered the cards.

They knelt in front of the fireplace. "I'm saving this one." Jack held up the jack of hearts he'd drawn. "I still don't believe it. Hey, do you remember that James Bond movie where he tried to seduce the fortune-teller and—"

His face froze and he stared at Laurel. Quickly, she raised her hand to toss the cards on the fire.

Jack grabbed her wrist. "—and there was only one card in the whole deck?" He tightened his grip until she released the cards.

They slithered to the floor in a waterfall—every one a jack of hearts.

Laurel was afraid to move.

"You cheated," he said, stunned.

"I prefer to think of it as hedging my bet."

Jack shot her an inscrutable look as he flipped each card faceup.

Why didn't he say something? "You said whatever happens," Laurel reminded him. "Are you going to keep your word?" She held her breath.

Jack looked at her, then his lips curved into a slow smile. He tossed the card he held over his shoulder and leaned toward her. "You bet."

CHAPTER TWELVE

"WHAT DO YOU MEAN, you're *not* wearing white!"

Holly winced after her outburst, though Laurel couldn't tell if it was in response to her announcement or because her sister was nine months pregnant and enduring a hot Dallas June.

She gestured to a pink cut-velvet love seat in the brides' dressing room at Neiman-Marcus. Holly sank onto it, surreptitiously rubbing her abdomen. Ivy edged the coffee table closer to Holly and placed a pillow on top.

"On the count of three," Laurel instructed, then she and Ivy each hoisted one of Holly's swollen legs onto the pillow.

Laurel raised her eyebrows as her sister focused on a distant point, breathing deeply and rhythmically. "More false labor?"

Holly nodded. "Dr. Hickman says it's perfectly normal and that I'm at least a week away from delivering." She tried to bend sideways, reaching for her clipboard, before giving up and holding out her hand. Ivy obediently supplied the clipboard. "A good thing, too. I don't have time to have a baby until after your wedding."

"Which, fortunately, is only two days from now."

"Yes." Holly tapped a pen on the clipboard. "Far too late for any jokes."

Laurel darted a glance at Ivy and swallowed. "It wasn't a joke." She sat on the love seat next to Holly.

"Of course it was," Holly insisted. "I ordered your dress weeks ago. Lovely candlelight satin with reembroidered alençon lace—"

"And I canceled the order weeks ago."

Holly's face froze. "You mean you changed the order?"

"Canceled," Laurel gently emphasized. There'd be enough screaming when Holly learned the rest.

There was silence and then, "You're eloping." Holly clutched her stomach.

"No. We'll be getting married at Central Presbyterian just as planned."

"But the dress was perfect—*and* it was on sale."

Laurel nodded her agreement. "The dress was gorgeous, but it wasn't...me."

Holly gripped the arms of the chair and drew a shuddering breath. "And what is *you?*"

"Oh, something more—" Laurel gestured nervously "—dramatic, more unusual. More..."

"Red," offered Ivy.

Laurel shot her a warning look, immediately intercepted by Holly.

"What have you done?"

Honestly, Laurel thought, it was *her* wedding, so why was she feeling so defensive about the changes she'd made?

"You know that Jack and I are opening the Hartman Agency in Los Angeles."

Holly nodded warily.

"Advertising is hideously expensive. I have no clients and no track record. I need a gimmick."

"Oh, no."

"Red has always been my color—"

"Oh, no." Holly's eyes widened.

"—and ties in nicely with the heart theme."

"What heart theme?" Holly asked with the beginnings of panic.

"You know, Hartman...hearts? The heart-shaped-diamond engagement ring?" Ivy explained. "I thought it was cute."

"I plan to wear red everywhere. It'll be my trademark," Laurel continued, hoping to stave off the impending explosion. "We've sent invitations to anyone who's anybody—"

"And a few people she'd like to make into somebody," Ivy inserted, earning her another warning glare from Laurel.

"We've leaked announcements to the press and *Variety*."

"What does Jack have to say about all this?" Accusation rang in Holly's voice.

"He helped write the press release." Laurel felt a thrill at the thought of Jack and the new life they'd planned together. "He's developed quite a talent for Hollywood hype."

"I see." Holly blinked. "Tell me about your wedding dress."

"Remember the red dress I wore to the New Year's Eve casino party? It's Jack's favorite."

"That doesn't mean you have to get married in it!"

"It was Jack's idea! In fact, he suggested that the designer add a matching train..."

Laurel's words trailed off as Holly closed her eyes and began deep-breathing exercises.

"More contractions?" Ivy asked.

"No, stress." Holly exhaled. "You are aware that the peach moiré Ivy and I are wearing does not complement red bugle beads?"

Laurel braced herself before replying, "I changed that, too."

Holly flung the clipboard to the floor and turned on Laurel. "How could you do this to me?"

"I haven't done anything to you. This is *my* wedding. You're having a baby. You've already had *your* wedding."

"Fortunately," murmured Ivy.

At that moment, the fitter knocked on the door and entered, carrying three garment bags.

Glad of the distraction, Laurel hurried to help the woman. "Don't worry so much, Holly." She unfastened the bags, exposing frothy white chiffon in two of them and her red dress in the third. "I doubled the order to the caterer and reserved a larger room at the hotel. I even remembered to coordinate the flowers."

Holly pointed a trembling finger. "White? I'm wearing white? I'm nine months pregnant and I'm wearing white?"

Laurel nodded and shook out the loosely cut, flowing gown. "Ivy is wearing the same dress. You see, the gathers under the bodice form folds that—"

"I know," Holly began in a martyred tone. "You couldn't get the Goodyear Blimp and decided to make do with my stomach!"

Laurel, holding on to her temper with great difficulty, let a little slip. "Well, I don't see any difference between being a peach blimp and a white blimp!"

She marched over to the hanging bag containing her wedding dress and the custom-designed veil. Viciously unzipping the dress she wore, Laurel wiggled into the tight, beaded column.

"Everyone's going to stare at me!" Holly wailed.

"No one's going to stare at you—*I'm* the bride." Laurel urged the dress over her hips and presented her back to the fitter. "And in this dress, I guarantee no one—"

"Ladies!" Ivy clapped her hands. "Holly, we need to hem your dress. Mine's already finished." She offered a hand to her sister. Holly struggled to her feet as Laurel hopped onto the raised platform.

The fitter settled a beaded headpiece and veil onto Laurel's head, and Holly smiled. "You'll never go through with it," she insisted.

"I CAN'T BELIEVE you're actually going through with it." Holly squirmed as the limousine rounded a corner.

"Smile, Holly!" Laurel waved and blew kisses to the photographers gathered in the evening light on the steps outside the church.

"I can't!" A sob caught in Holly's throat. "I'll look like a beached whale trying to climb out of this vulgar car!"

"Since when are white limousines vulgar?"

"Since you pasted red hearts on the side."

"Oh, piffle! Ivy, do you have the press releases?"

"Right here. Holly, can you make it up the steps while I distribute these, or shall I ask the driver to help you?"

Holly moaned. "This isn't a wedding, it's a publicity stunt."

"Jack and I are starting our new life together. We wanted the whole world to know."

"No problem there," Ivy muttered.

Laurel turned away from the window as the driver approached her door. "Marriage is only one purpose of a wedding. Every bride learns that."

"You obviously learned your lesson well." Holly bit off the last word.

Laurel regarded her sister closely. "Are you sure this isn't too much for you? You should've let us hold the wedding a month ago."

"No. There wouldn't have been time—but then, you changed everything around, anyway." Holly winced. "I'm sorry I'm such a grump, but I haven't rested once today, I didn't eat much dinner, and it seems like I've had one episode of these stupid contractions after another."

"Oh, Holly, why didn't you say something?" Remorse filled Laurel's voice.

Her sister squeezed her hand. "This is your day. I didn't want to spoil it for you." She touched the glittering diamond necklace Laurel wore. "Mama's necklace looks great, even with that dress."

Laurel glanced down at the three strands set with huge, fake diamonds. "It would take a lot to upstage this necklace."

The driver opened the door and Laurel grinned at her sisters. "Come on. I don't want to keep Jack waiting!"

"This way, Ms. Hall!"

Laurel smiled into a blizzard of flashes. She hitched up her dress and climbed the steps, her veil billowing in a red mist behind her.

Jack, clad in a black tuxedo, red tie and cummerbund, waited at the top of the stone steps. Though they'd planned this moment as a photo opportunity, one look into his amused green eyes, and Laurel was lost all over again. She forgot the photographers and her sisters. Forgot about publicity and potential clients. There was only her handsome soon-to-be husband holding out his hand to her.

She reached toward him and felt his energizing warmth as she grabbed a hold of him and her future.

"I *love* that dress," he whispered, tucking her hand around his arm. "But not nearly as much as I love the woman who's wearing it."

Jack's expression enthralled her, and it took his gentle nudge to remind her where they were.

As they entered the church narthex, the florist thrust a bouquet of white heart-shaped anthurium into her arms. The string quartet began the processional music and Laurel and Jack, preceded by Laurel's sisters carrying bouquets of red anthurium, walked slowly down the aisle.

For Laurel, the ceremony was a jumble of impressions: the shocked hush, then the babble of voices as they made their entrance, the catch in Jack's voice as he repeated his vows, Holly's constant fidgeting and Adam's frequent glances at his wife.

Her unconventional attire forgotten, Laurel found herself profoundly moved by the words of the ceremony. During her marriage, she expected good times—even great times—as well as difficult times, but she had no doubt that she and Jack would live happily ever after.

And then the service was over, and she and Jack and Ivy were hugging each other in the narthex.

"Where are Holly and Adam?" Ivy asked, turning around. "Didn't they follow us out?"

Jack and Laurel looked at each other, then back into the sanctuary. Their wedding guests remained standing, gazes riveted on the front of the church.

They hurried forward to find Holly doubled over in a pew, Adam kneeling beside her. "We need to get her to the hospital. She's in labor and, from what I understand, has been most of the day."

"Sorry, Laur—" Holly broke off to pant.

"She made it through the ceremony, then relaxed and..." Adam gestured vaguely, sweat beading his lip.

"Let's carry her into the limousine," Jack suggested.

Holly began to struggle. "Not that car! I'm not going to chance giving birth in that tasteless piece of—"

"Good idea," Adam said.

"*Great* idea, Holly!" Laurel gave her sister a thumbs-up. "Think of the publicity!"

Immediately following the ceremony, the matron of honor was rushed to West Side Hospital where she gave birth to a nine-pound, two-ounce boy. Mother and son are doing fine. The bride and groom, at present honeymooning on an undisclosed Caribbean island, will return to Los Angeles for the opening of the Hartman Agency on August 1.

Laurel tapped the newspaper. "Wasn't Holly a trooper to have Nicholas when she did? I'm telling you, Jack, you can't buy publicity like this."

"Somehow, I don't think that occurred to her." Jack squirted suntan lotion onto his palms and began rubbing Laurel's shoulders. Sheets of newspaper whispered to the sand.

Laurel closed her eyes. "Changing the subject?"

"We're alone on a beach on a tropical island, and we've only been married for two days." Jack turned her to face him. "I think we're talking entirely too much, Mrs. Hartman," he said, pulling her insistently toward him.

"I think you're right, Mr. Hartman," Laurel murmured as his lips met hers.

What's in the cards for Ivy,
the youngest Hall sister?
Watch for Heather Allison's next
Harlequin Romance, Ivy's League,
coming in 1993.

BARBARY WHARF

**An exciting six-book series, one title per month
beginning in October, by bestselling author**

Set in the glamorous and fast-paced world of international
journalism, BARBARY WHARF will take you from the
Sentinel's hectic newsroom to the most thrilling cities in the
world. You'll meet media tycoon Nick Caspian and his
adversary Gina Tyrrell, whose dramatic story of passion and
heartache develops throughout the six-book series.

In book one, BESIEGED (#1498), you'll also meet Hazel and
Piet. Hazel's always had a good word to say about everyone.
Well, almost. She just can't stand Piet Van Leyden, Nick's
chief architect and one of the most arrogant know-it-alls she's
ever met! As far as Hazel's concerned, Piet's a twentieth-
century warrior, and she's the one being besieged!

Don't miss the sparks in the first BARBARY WHARF
book, BESIEGED (#1498), available in October from
Harlequin Presents.

BARB-S

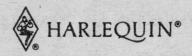

THE TAGGARTS OF TEXAS!

Harlequin's Ruth Jean Dale brings you
THE TAGGARTS OF TEXAS!

Those Taggart men—strong, sexy and hard to resist...

You've met Jesse James Taggart in FIREWORKS!
Harlequin Romance #3205 (July 1992)

Now meet Trey Smith—he's THE RED-BLOODED YANKEE!
Harlequin Temptation #413 (October 1992)

Then there's Daniel Boone Taggart in SHOWDOWN!
Harlequin Romance #3242 (January 1993)

And finally the Taggarts who started it all—in LEGEND!
Harlequin Historical #168 (April 1993)

Read all the Taggart romances!
Meet all the Taggart men!

Available wherever Harlequin books are sold.